More Irish Fairy Tales

Sinéad de Valera was married to the former Irish President, and died early in 1975 at the age of ninety-six. She wrote several books of Irish fairy tales for children. In this selection of ten stories Mrs de Valera tells of witches and fairies, magic and spells. All have an element of fantasy, and all are original yet steeped in tradition.

Also by
Sinéad de Valera in Piccolo

Irish Fairy Tales

Sinéad de Valera

More Irish Fairy Tales

text illustrations by Julek Heller

Piper
PAN MACMILLAN
CHILDREN'S BOOKS

The stories in this collection were selected from
The Verdant Valley, The Emerald Ring, The Stolen Child,
Fairy Tales and *The Four-Leaved Shamrock* by Sinéad de Valera,
published by C. J. Fallon Ltd, Dublin
This Piper Book collection published 1979 by Pan Macmillan Children's Books Ltd,
a division of Pan Macmillan Limited,
Cavaye Place, London SW10 9PG
10 12 14 16 18 19 17 15 13 11
This collection © C. J. Fallon Ltd 1979
ISBN 0 330 25669 6
Printed in England by Clays Ltd, St Ives plc

Contents

The Magic Thorn

Once upon a time, there lived near the coast of Clare a rich widow named Ina. She had one child, a girl called Aisling. At about two miles' distance from their home was another castle. Strange to relate the occupants were also a widow and her daughter. The mother's name was Alna. The girl was called Cliona.

Aisling and Cliona grew up together and were friends. Alna, however, watched with jealous eyes the difference between them. Aisling was very beautiful and had a gentle, affectionate disposition. She was a talented musician, too, and was beloved by everyone. Cliona, on the other hand, had no pretensions to good looks. She was plain and had an unfriendly manner.

Midway between the two houses there was a great castle. In it lived an eccentric old man named Kian. For months at a time he would not speak to anyone nor allow visitors to come near his house. Then he would go to the other extreme and ask the young people of the surrounding countryside to come and spend hours dancing, singing and having a really good time. He himself always took part in the festivities. He sang, though his old voice was cracked. He danced, always selecting the smallest partner, though he himself was well over six feet in height. He often had to be assisted to his feet after trying to give a display in tumbling. When hurling, he hit everything but the ball.

The young people loved him, but they could not refrain from laughing at his strange ways and manners. In the household was an elderly man named Eoin. He had known Kian since they were both boys. There was great affection between servant and master. After a period of absence and isolation, Kian called Eoin to him—

'I would like to invite a number of people to a great ball.'

'Oh! yes,' said Eoin: 'Aisling could give great delight to all by playing the harp.'

'Yes, but I don't want to tire her by asking her to play all the time.'

'Don't worry about that point, dear master. I can get you another harpist.'

'Oh! Eoin, you are a genius, but where or when can you get one?'

'As I was passing by a house today I heard music coming from inside. As I knew the people of the house I went in. There, seated in the midst of the family was a young man playing the harp. The father, mother and children were listening with delight. The music was so entrancing I stayed to hear more. When I was leaving the man of the house came out with me. "Who is that harpist?" I asked him. "O! indeed," said he, "his is a sad story. He should be rich and happy, for his parents were wealthy but both of them were careless and extravagant. They are now dead and their poor son has no means of living except by playing the harp."'

Kian started up. 'Get the horse and car at once, Eoin,' he said, 'and go to that house and bring the harpist here.' In a short time Eoin returned with the harpist.

'You are welcome,' said Kian. 'Please tell me your name.'

'Connla is my name.'

'Now, Eoin,' said Kian, 'before anything else, see that Connla gets a good meal. Then after he has had a rest bring him back here to me.'

After a time Eoin brought Connla to the room where Kian awaited him.

'Now, please, let me hear you play,' said the old man, as he looked kindly at the harpist.

Kian listened with delight, indeed, almost with rapture to the sweet music. Then he rose from his seat and grasped Connla's hand.

'Oh! please make your home here with me,' he said, 'your music will be a source of constant pleasure.'

'But,' answered Connla, 'my music would be but a small return for the luxury of living in such a home as this.'

'It will be a big return. It will bring joy to my heart and will brighten my life.'

Both were well pleased with the arrangement; Kian with the joy of having music in the house; Connla with the thought of having ease and comfort in a good home.

The invitations were sent out. The ball room was a scene of grandeur and beauty. Old Kian himself was in high spirits. The young people loved him but they could hardly restrain their laughter at his extraordinary appearance. His robe of many colours descended from his neck to his feet. He had a crown of bright flowers on his head, but the most comical part of his costume was a broad red ribbon tied at the end of his long, grey beard.

'Now, my friends,' said he, 'before the dancing begins I would like to speak to you all.' He took Aisling by the hand.

'Here,' said he, 'is the harpist who will give us sweet music.' There was loud applause.

'Now,' continued Kian as he led Connla forward, 'here is another harpist who, with Aisling, will set your twinkling feet dancing with delight. I wish to tell you he is my adopted son and he will inherit all I possess.'

The audience were for a moment silent. Then there were cries of joy and congratulation. The music began. There were other musicians present. Dance followed dance. Connla had just finished dancing with Aisling when he said – 'You will keep the next dance for me.'

'Oh no, please ask my friend, Cliona, to dance. No one has asked her yet.'

'Very well, but you will keep the next for me.'

'Yes.'

The time passed joyfully and all were loud in their thanks to their kind host. There was one, however, who did not share in the general happiness. This was Cliona. When she arrived home, her mother saw at once from her looks that she was sullen and discontented.

'Did you not enjoy the ball?' asked the mother.

'No, indeed, mother. Aisling deprived me of all pleasure. Everyone was anxious to dance with the harpist but she kept him all to herself.'

'Who is the harpist?'

'He is a handsome young man and a splendid musician. Kian has taken a great interest in him, so much so that he has made him heir to all his possessions.'

'And you say this harpist paid particular attention to Aisling?'

'Yes, and he hardly noticed me.'

'That girl seems to be always interfering with your happiness.'

'Yes, indeed, mother, only for her I would receive much more attention.'

'Well, we must be patient and pretend to be friendly with her. You know Kian is very fond of her and we must not do anything to displease him.'

Kian was so much pleased with the success of the ball he determined to organize other forms of amusement. His next plan was to have a swimming competition. The day was somewhat chilly but the young folk determined to have their fun. Of course, Kian said he would take part in the contest.

'But, master dear,' said Eoin, 'the weather is cold.'

'Cold or not I am going to swim,' was Kian's answer.

He was not long in the water till he called for help. Eoin was watching from the shore. When he heard his loved master's call he dashed into the sea. Both had to be rescued. They were brought from the water exhausted and almost unconscious. All care was given them but the shock had been too great. Eoin insisted that his bed should be placed beside that of his loved master. Hour by hour they grew weaker till at the dawn of a bright, spring day Kian died. Some hours after, Eoin passed away. It seemed as if he could not stay when his beloved master was gone.

Connla was much grieved by the death of him who had shown him such generous kindness. Aisling, too, felt that one of her dearest friends had gone from her. She had from childhood known and loved him. For a long time his loss was felt throughout the neighbourhood.

After some time news of another kind went round. Joyful news it was. Connla and Aisling were going to be married. The news brought joy to all hearts except those of Alna and Cliona.

'That girl has stood between me and happiness throughout our lives,' said Cliona.

'Yes, indeed, my child,' was her mother's reply, 'only for her Connla would have married you.'

'If we could get her away from here, mother, I am sure

he would forget her but the fairies themselves would find it hard to banish her.'

'Talking of the fairies,' said Alna, 'what about the witch of the cave?'

'Oh! mother, you are a genius, perhaps the witch could help us.'

'Well, Cliona, we had better hurry and see her for the wedding is to take place very soon.'

'Where is the witch's home?'

'It is in a cave at the foot of the cliffs. We would have to climb to the top of the cliffs at this side and descend on the other. I believe the witch can be seen at midnight only.'

'Then, mother, we should set out as soon as possible.'

That night the wicked pair started off. They had to climb up the cliffs and then walk along a narrow path overlooking the sea. They then descended by a winding way and came to a sort of cave.

The witch heard them approaching. She came to the opening of the cave. She held a rushlight which gave faint light amid the almost black darkness. Such an ugly, wicked, old creature! Her nose and chin almost met and her eyes were like balls of fire.

'Who comes here?' she asked.

'Friends,' said Alna.

'Aye, friends that want something,' snarled the witch.

'Yes, we want your help.'

'My help must be paid for.'

'Yes, we understand that. May we come into your house and rest a while? We are weary after the long walk on the cliff path.'

'No. You cannot come in. No one is ever allowed to enter my house. Now tell me what you want.'

'My daughter here is anxious to marry a certain man.'

'And why does she not marry him?'

'Because he intends marrying another girl.'

'Oh! I understand. He would marry your daughter if the other girl were out of the way.'

'Yes.'

'Well, I could get her out of the way if you are willing to pay the price I ask.'

'What is the price?'

'That you give me your most precious possession.'

Alna thought for a while. Then she said – 'My most precious possession is a beautiful mirror framed in gold. It would be hard to part with it.'

'Well, it is the price of my service to you. Without it I will not help you.'

'Oh! mother,' said Cliona, 'do please give the mirror.'

'I suppose I must, Cliona.'

'Yes, you must if you wish to get my help,' said the witch.

'Then I must part with my treasure.'

'Yes,' said the witch. 'Now when was this wedding to take place?'

'In a few days' time,' Cliona answered.

'Then come with me, we must act quickly.'

The witch led them to a small patch of land on which was a little bush. She plucked a thorn from the bush and handed it to Cliona.

'Now,' she said. 'Insert the thorn into the girl's arm. She will immediately look as if she were dead.'

'How long will she remain as a corpse?' asked Alna.

'As long as I live,' said the witch with a wicked chuckle, 'and that will be a long, long time indeed. At my death the thorn will disappear unseen by mortal eyes. Now at the midnight of the day after tomorrow I will go to your house and bring the mirror here.'

'But it is very heavy,' said Alna.

'Well, you two can come with me and we will carry it in turns. Begone now!'

The two wicked women departed, well pleased with their visit. Next morning, Cliona went to Aisling's house.

'Aisling,' she said, 'come with me for a walk through the fields. The day is lovely. You know we cannot have another walk together for some time.'

Everything was beautiful in the clear morning air. Primroses and violets were to be seen on all sides. Young leaves were opening on the trees. The happy birds answered each other in song.

'Oh! what a beautiful world this is!' said Aisling, as she stooped to gather some violets. Like a flash, Cliona pushed the thorn into her arm. Poor Aisling fell to the ground. Cliona ran quickly into the house in what seemed to be a state of great agitation.

'Oh! come, come quickly,' she said. 'Aisling is dead.'

She plucked a thorn from the bush and handed it to Cliona

Oh! the misery and the sorrow! Doctors were summoned. Every remedy was tried. All in vain. What had been a happy home was now one of sorrow and despair.

None were louder in the expression of grief and sympathy than the wicked pair, Alna and Cliona. They stayed for many hours in the desolate home. They came again next morning but could not remain far into the night as they had to keep their appointment with the witch.

She came at midnight. She was much pleased when she saw the exquisite mirror. 'I made a good bargain,' she thought to herself.

'Now, my friends, we had better hurry for I see some signs of a fog.'

They started off taking turns of carrying the mirror. They managed to climb to the top of the cliffs. The fog was now more dense. They went on, one by one, Alna first, then the witch, then Cliona. They had made some headway when the witch struck her foot against a large stone. She stumbled. The mirror fell from her hands and crashed on the rocks below. In rage and disappointment she stretched out her arms and caught hold of the other two. There was a struggle which ended in all three falling as the mirror had done. The outgoing tide bore their bodies far away out to sea. They were never heard of more.

Just at this time, Sile, Aisling's old nurse, was keeping vigil by the bedside of the one she had loved so well. She had lost much sleep. For a moment her eyes closed.

Suddenly she started up in amazement and almost terror when she heard her name called in her loved child's voice, 'Sile.' There was Aisling sitting up in bed. Sile rushed into the nearby room.

'Come, come quickly,' she said to the mother and some friends who were there, Connla amongst them.

Oh! the wonder and the rapture!

Aisling could give no account of what had happened. She remembered stooping to pick the flowers. After that her mind was a blank. For miles round wonder and amazement spread among all who heard of what seemed to be a miraculous occurrence. Aisling was beloved by young and old. The sorrow caused by her apparent death was well outweighed by her happy return to life.

Some months after the strange events there was a magnificent wedding. Connla and Aisling had many children. Among them were twin boys named Kian and Eoin.

The disappearance of Alna and Cliona was a nine days' wonder. Since they had never won affection or esteem they left no happy memories after them.

The Disguised Princess

Princess Eithne lived in a fine palace with her mother, Queen Rose, and her stepfather King Conal. Eithne disliked her stepfather very much because he was a harsh and cruel man.

Queen Rose died and the princess was very lonely after her death. One day King Conal sent a message to Princess Eithne to come at once to the throne room. The princess wondered what her stepfather could want with her, but she did as he asked.

When she reached the throne room she was surprised to find a tall, dark stranger with King Conal and when the stranger turned to face her, she saw he had a very ugly, wicked face.

'This is Prince Igon who is going to marry you,' said King Conal. 'He is a great friend of mine so you must do as I say.'

The poor girl was very unhappy. She had a beautiful mare who she thought was the creature in all the world that loved her best, so she told this mare her sad story.

The mare was really a fairy in disguise and she was a sort of guardian to this princess. To her surprise, the mare spoke to Eithne and told her this: 'Don't be uneasy,' she added. 'I will help you. Tell your stepfather that you will not marry till you get a dress made of silk and silver thread and that the dress must fit into a walnut shell. I will delay the workers so that he will be kept a long time waiting.'

Princess Eithne did as her friend, the mare, told her and asked King Conal for a dress made of silk and silver thread that would fit into a walnut shell.

He didn't like the marriage to be delayed, but he yielded to her wishes and ordered the court dressmakers to make it as quickly as they could. They worked hard at their sewing, but something seemed to delay them every day and so the dress wasn't ready for many months. When the dress was finished the King thought that Princess Eithne would marry Prince Igon, but on the mare's advice she told him she wanted another dress – this time one made of silk and gold thread and that it, too, must fit into a walnut shell.

Again the mare worked her magic and the making of the dress was very slow, but it was finished at last.

'Surely,' said King Conal, 'you will marry Igon now.'

'I will not marry,' said Princess Eithne, 'till I get a dress of silk thread covered with pearls and diamonds. It, too, must fit into a walnut shell.'

King Conal was disappointed and angry but he ordered the dress for her. 'This is the last one you will get,' he said.

After a long delay the dress was ready, but at the same time the mare gave Eithne a dress of cat-skins. The princess put this on and put the three walnuts in her pocket. On the advice of the mare she stained her face and hands with a brown colour and in this disguise she mounted on the mare and before daybreak they were miles away from the palace.

They reached a wood and Eithne dismounted. She sat down under a shady tree, and was soon in a sound sleep. Suddenly she was awakened by the barking and yelping of dogs. They looked very fierce when they saw the cat-skins, but a hunter came up and called them to him. The hunter was none other than King Brian who was famous throughout the land for his valour and kindness. He thought the princess was a very pretty girl, but wondered at her strange colour and the extraordinary dress she wore. When he found that she was alone and friendless he brought her to the palace and gave orders that she should be employed in the kitchen.

The other servants laughed at Eithne's strange dress and called her 'Cat-skins'. She was given a very, very small bedroom far away from the other apartments.

To the great surprise and annoyance of the household King Brian asked that Cat-skins should be his own personal attendant. When she came into his presence he asked her many questions, but though he knew from her voice and manner that she was of noble birth he could get very little information from her.

The hunter was none other than King Brian

One night King Brian attended a great ball in a nearby castle. That same night, the princess, having washed the stain from her face and hands, went to bed early. She could not sleep, however, and rose and went out in the cool air. What should she see but the mare under a tree. The mare told her to open the first walnut shell.

'Now,' said the mare, 'hold the dress over your head and put it on.'

When Eithne was clothed in the beautiful silk and silver dress the mare, who wore fine harness, told her to mount on her back. Off they galloped and soon they arrived at the castle where the ball was being held.

Everyone was amazed when the beautifully dressed girl entered. King Brian came forward to meet her and spent the rest of the night by her side. He was very sorry when she said she must go home and wished that she would allow his servants to attend her on the way. She told him she preferred to go alone and that the mare was waiting for her. He helped her into the saddle and she was off like a flash.

Next morning Princess Eithne put on her cat-skin dress and stained her hands and face.

The King sent for her. While she was working he looked at her and thought that but for the colour of her skin, she looked very like the beautiful lady who had come to the ball. He questioned her about her home and people, but her answers told him very little.

In a short time there was another great ball. King

Brian went to it and when he had gone, Eithne put on her silk and gold dress and mounting her friend the mare, she followed him there. She looked even more beautiful than she did at the first ball and the King fell more deeply in love with her. When she was leaving he again begged to be let accompany her, but Eithne told him that she preferred to go alone. However, she promised him that she would come to the next ball which was to be held a week later.

In the morning when she was sewing a button on the King's cuff he noticed how small and well-shaped was her hand, but when he questioned her she finished her work quickly and hurried away.

At the third ball Princess Eithne was dazzlingly beautiful in her dress of silk with the pearls and diamonds. King Brian wished to accompany her to her home and was very sad when she again said that she must go alone.

'However,' the princess said, 'if you know me next time you see me we shall never part again.'

When she was seated on the mare, King Brian managed to slip a very small ring on her finger without her noticing it.

Next morning he sent for her. He told her that he wished to ask her opinion about certain clothes as he was going to be married. Eithne said that a poor girl like her could not advise him and that he had better consult the beautiful lady about whom all the servants were talking.

'I suppose she will be your bride,' she said.

'It is just as probable that you will be my bride,' said King Brian.

'I your bride!' Eithne said.

'Yes, because you and the beautiful lady are one. That ring on your finger tells me so. You promised we would part no more if I knew you the next time we met. I claim you now as my bride.'

Princess Eithne went out hurriedly and returned in a short time. She had washed off the brown stain and put on her dress of silk and jewels.

'Now,' she said when she came back, 'I'm fit to be your bride.'

The marriage took place almost immediately and one of the principal guests was the fairy who had disguised herself as the mare and who now appeared as a beautiful woman.

The wedding feast lasted for three days and three nights and King Brian and his bride lived happily ever after.

The Emerald Ring

Once upon a time there lived in Munster a king named Mahon with his queen, Una. They had a beautiful daughter named Emer. Suitors came from all parts of Eirinn and even from beyond the sea to seek her hand in marriage. Emer, however, had made her own choice.

'I will marry no one but Flan, the young King of Connacht,' she said.

'In my opinion,' declared King Mahon, 'you could not find a better husband and I am sure that is your mother's opinion, too.'

'Indeed it is,' said the queen.

The wedding preparations began at once.

One day the queen called her daughter to her and said:

'This emerald ring which I constantly wear was given to me by my mother a short time before my marriage. I shall now give it to you as a wedding gift.'

'Oh, thank you, Mother!' said Emer, 'I have always liked that ring and I think it is very beautiful.'

'It is beautiful,' replied the queen, 'but it is valuable for another reason as well as for its beauty. It has the power to protect you from harm. If your life is ever threatened by an enemy, the emerald will become black as night to warn you that danger is near.'

'I do not think I have any enemy, Mother, but I shall wear the ring night and day and shall treasure it beyond all my gifts.'

Now there was a princess in Connacht named Maeve who wished to marry King Flan. When she found out that a wedding was arranged between him and Emer, she became nearly mad with jealousy. She set out at once for Munster. Here she lived in a little hut hidden among a clump of bushes. A well near by supplied her with water and she had brought provisions with her when she was leaving home. The hut was not far from King Mahon's castle. She hoped to find out all about the wedding preparations and to discover some way of preventing the marriage.

Unfortunately, anyone who is determined to commit an evil deed will always find means to do it.

One day Maeve wandered far away from all human habitation until she came to a forest. As she went farther in among the trees, she could hardly see the way but the darkness suited her gloomy and wicked thoughts. All at once she heard a harsh, grating laugh. The sound seemed to come from the top of one of the trees. She looked up. There, sitting on one of the highest branches, was a hideously ugly old hag with a lantern in her hand. She wore a long black cloak with a hood. From out of the

The hag flew down to where Maeve stood

hood her grey hair streamed almost into her eyes. Turning the light of the lantern on Maeve's upturned face, she said: 'You look unhappy, fair stranger. What is your trouble?'

'I am unhappy,' said Maeve, 'and I cannot find anyone to help me to do as I wish.'

'What is it that you wish?' asked the hag.

'I wish to prevent the marriage of King Flan and Princess Emer.'

'Oh!' said the hag, 'come home with me and I shall tell you how that can be done.'

As she said these words she spread out her cloak while still holding the lantern in her right hand. The cloak took the form of two great black wings and the hag flew down to where Maeve stood. Together they went through the wood till they came out at the farther end. There Maeve saw an enormous flat stone lying on the ground. By the far side of the stone a river came hurrying down over some rocks and formed a waterfall. On the side near the wood there was a kind of trap-door. The hag knocked at this door with a rod of birch which she had taken from a tree as she passed through the wood. Immediately the door flew open and there before them was an ugly old man. He stood at the top of a flight of stone steps which led to a large room beneath. This room was lighted by lanterns hanging on the walls.

'Well, Wife, who is this stranger?' asked the old man.

'Wait till we go down to the room,' said the hag, 'and I will tell you all about her.'

The three descended into the stone chamber. It was cold and bare and the noise of river at the far end was so great that Maeve feared the water would burst through and drown them all.

When the hag had told her husband what Maeve wished, he said to his wife, 'And what reward will you expect from this woman, if you are able to grant her desire to prevent the marriage?'

'She must get for me the queen's golden mirror and the silver comb of the princess. Then I can comb my hair and keep it from falling into my eyes.'

'And what am I to get?' asked the man. 'I would like the king's slippers because my feet are sore from running up and down the stone steps.'

'Very well,' said the hag. Then she turned to Maeve and said: 'If you promise to get these three things for us, I shall tell you how you can prevent the marriage.'

'But how can I get these things?'

'That you must find out for yourself, but I shall lend you my cloak which will enable you to escape capture if you are pursued. When you have secured the slippers, mirror and comb, hide them safely in your hut. Now listen to my plan for bringing about the death of the princess. Take this pear. It seems to be delicious but inside is a worm which will cause the death of anyone who eats the fruit. If you can manage to get the Princess Emer to eat it, she will trouble you no longer.'

'I will at least do my best to make her eat it,' said Maeve.

'If you fail, there is another way to bring about her death. I know she often sits under a large beech tree in the garden. Take this little axe. It is small but it has wonderful power. Watch till you see the princess coming to sit under the tree. Then strike the trunk near the roots. The tree will fall a short time after you have struck it. You can fly away to safety. The axe can be used only once. It will turn to powder in your hand after you have cut the tree. Now listen to me attentively.'

'I am listening,' said Maeve, 'and I am very thankful for your help.'

'Fearing by some chance,' continued the hag, 'this second plan should fail, I shall tell you of another one. Emer sometimes walks alone by the lake side. Wait in hiding near the deepest part of the water. Spring out suddenly and push her into the lake. She will be drowned before help can come and your wings will carry you safely away. Now go and return here with the slippers, mirror and comb, after you have succeeded in killing the princess. Take this birch rod. Knock on the trap-door when you return and it will spring open.'

The old man led Maeve up the steps and the hag brought her through the wood.

All this time the wedding preparations were going on.

Maeve returned to the hut and remained there a couple of days. She stayed inside till the second nightfall and then she went towards the castle to see if she could find some way of getting inside the gates. She noticed that the king and queen with their daughter came out at night to walk in the moonlight.

On the third night after her return, Maeve disguised herself as a beggar woman and went to the castle gates. She waited there for the king and his wife and daughter to come out. She had put on the hag's cloak and under it she carried a bag.

When she saw King Mahon approaching with the queen and princess she crouched down by the castle gates and began to moan and cry.

'Oh! Look at that poor creature,' said the princess.

The king and queen drew near Maeve and asked her what was the matter.

'Oh! Your Majesties,' she exclaimed, 'I am homeless, hungry and desolate.'

'Poor creature,' said the queen, 'we must help her.'

'Here, Fergal,' said the king to one of his attendants, 'take this woman to the kitchen and see that she gets a good meal and give orders to have a bed prepared for her.'

Maeve was loud in her thanks as she followed the attendant. After a while, when all the servants were at supper, she stole quietly to the king's bedroom. There she found the slippers. She put them in the bag. Next she took the golden mirror from the queen's table and then she went to Emer's room and found the silver comb. There was a basket of fruit on the table and in it she placed the pear. She then opened wide the great window and, spreading out the cloak, flew into the night.

When Emer and her father and mother went to their rooms, they were greatly surprised and vexed to find the slippers, mirror and comb were missing.

Emer went to the table to get some fruit and saw the beautiful pear. She was about to eat it when she noticed that the emerald ring had turned black. She opened the pear and saw a horrible worm inside. In fear and disgust she cast the fruit through the open window. When her mother came in to say good night to her she found her pale and trembling.

'Oh, Mother!' she exclaimed. 'The ring has saved me! I must have an enemy, after all.'

'Who can your enemy be, my child?'

'I believe, Mother, it is that beggar woman. I am sure it was she who left a pear with a horrible worm inside it among the fruit on my table. As I was about to eat it, the emerald turned black and warned me of the danger.'

'Don't be uneasy, Emer; your ring will preserve you from harm.'

Next morning, Maeve kept watch from a hill near the castle to see if Emer would appear. To her rage and disappointment, she saw the princess come out on horseback, accompanied by King Flan.

'She has not eaten the pear,' thought Maeve. She kept a close watch on the castle grounds every day and one morning she saw Emer come out and walk in the direction of the beech tree. She flew at once towards the tree and cut the trunk with the axe. The axe immediately crumbled to dust in her hand. The foliage on the tree was so thick that no one saw her approaching.

Emer came slowly, but when she was a little distance from the tree she saw the emerald turn black. She stood for a moment looking round her, when suddenly she heard a fearful crash and saw the giant tree fall to the earth.

'This again must be the work of my enemy. But for my ring I would have been killed,' she said to her attendant.

Only one chance to kill Emer now remained to the wicked Maeve. She waited day after day until at last she saw Emer walking alone by the side of the lake. She hid behind some bushes just opposite the deepest part of the water. As Emer came nearer to this point she noticed the emerald becoming darker and darker. She stopped. Maeve sprang from her hiding place, but suddenly she was caught and held fast by a pair of strong arms. Flan had come by a short cut across the fields to join Emer. He saw Maeve crouching down behind the bushes and when she darted out, he followed her and was just in time to save the princess.

The cloak slipped from Maeve's shoulders and to his amazement Flan recognized her.

'At last,' he said to Emer, 'we have discovered who your enemy is.'

'Oh! why have you tried to kill me?' said Emer. 'I have never injured you.'

'We will say no more now,' said Flan, 'but you, Maeve, will come with us to the castle.'

When Maeve was led into the presence of King Mahon and the queen her fear and shame were so great that she confessed all.

'And where now,' asked the king, 'are the things you have stolen?'

'If Your Majesty will have a guard sent with me, I will show you the hut where I have hidden them.'

'That will be done when you have told us where we shall find the hag's dwelling place.'

'It is far from here. First we must pass through a dark wood. The men must take lanterns to light them through the darkest part. At the far end of the wood is the stone dwelling of the hag and her husband.'

That evening Maeve brought the guards to the hut. All the lost articles were recovered. Shortly after the men had returned to the palace a fearful rainstorm came on. In the morning all the streams and rivers were swollen but as the day advanced the weather became fine.

Towards midday King Mahon and King Flan set out for the hag's dwelling, accompanied by a large number of attendants. Flan carried the hag's cloak, for he now knew what magic power it possessed and he feared Maeve would try to fly away.

When they came out of the wood and reached the

great stone, the king ordered Maeve to knock on the trap-door with the birch rod. When she knocked the door opened but inside, instead of the steps and stone chamber, they saw a deep lake.

'Oh, I know what has happened!' Maeve exclaimed. 'The water in the rushing river has broken down the wall at the far end of the chamber.'

'But where are the hag and her husband?' asked the king.

'I am sure, Your Majesty, they have been drowned in the lake and their bodies have been carried away in the rising waters.'

Flan leaned over to look at the lake. The cloak fell from his grasp. Maeve sprang forward to catch it but missed her footing and fell into the depths of the water. She was carried swiftly away by the rushing river. The king and all those with him were shocked to think of her fearful fate. They, like the queen and princess, had forgiven her for all the evil she had done.

In due course, Flan and Emer were married and lived happily ever after.

Emer kept the emerald ring with great care and never parted with it till her daughter Nora was about to be married. Nora in turn gave it to her daughter and in this way it remained in the family as a treasure and a protection against danger.

The Wishing Chair

(A story of the Olden Time)

'We are a happy family,' said Shane MacFadden, as he and his wife and daughter Roisin were having their supper one fine summer evening.

'Yes, indeed, Shane,' said his wife, 'but you have to work hard to keep us in such comfort.'

'You know, Nora, I am well helped by you and Roisin.'

'And, Father,' said Roisin, 'you also have managed to give me a good education and the opportunity to learn to play the harp.'

Roisin gave much pleasure to her parents by playing for them in the long winter evenings.

They were indeed a happy family with no thought of the trouble that was to come to them.

Sickness broke out in the neighbourhood. The inmates of the little house did not escape. Both father and mother died. Roisin recovered. A sad and lonely girl she was.

Her aunt, who lived some distance away, said she would leave her own house and come with her two daughters to live with her.

'I will be a mother to you, Roisin,' she said, 'and Mella and Gobnait will be just the same as sisters.'

It was a sad day for Roisin that the three women came to the house. All three were lazy and idle. They left all the work to Roisin.

The two girls were always arguing and quarrelling.

'I am tired of this life,' Mella said one day. 'I wish some handsome, rich man would come and marry me.'

'You with your yellow face and long, lanky figure the wife of a rich, handsome man!' said Gobnait.

'Well, Gobnait, I would rather have my nice, slight figure than be a fat, heavy creature like you. It is well you have such huge feet for if they were small they would never support your big, bulky body. If you did not eat so much you might have a nice, slight figure like mine.'

Roisin tried to make peace between them.

'You would both be much happier if you did not quarrel so much,' she said.

'Oh, you need not talk, Roisin,' said Mella. 'Everyone loves you.'

'Yes,' added Gobnait, 'and with your beauty you prevent anyone from looking at either of us.'

'You were lucky, too, in having had such devoted parents and in getting a good education.'

'Our parents took very little care with our upbringing,' said Mella. 'Even now my mother does not bother about us. She is either dozing at the fire or talking to the neighbours.'

There was neither peace nor comfort in the house and Roisin was very unhappy.

One night the sisters were looking out the window while their mother was sitting at the fire. Roisin was trying to tidy the kitchen.

'There is the new moon,' said Gobnait. 'I see it clear in the sky and not through a tree. Perhaps it will bring me good luck.'

'I don't care about the moon,' was Mella's remark. 'It never brought good luck to me.'

'Oh, look!' exclaimed Gobnait as a woman passed by the window, 'there is Ana Criona (wise Ana). I will call her in. She has always plenty of news.'

The woman, as her name implied, was believed to be very wise. She had wonderful stories of the olden time. For miles round she was welcomed in the different houses, but she never stayed longer than a couple of days in each.

'*Cead mile failte* (a hundred thousand welcomes), Ana,' said Roisin as she placed a chair near the fire.

'Though the day was warm the evening is chilly,' said Ana, 'and for an old woman like me the heat is pleasant.'

'Well, Ana, what news have you tonight?' asked Gobnait.

'Good news,' Ana replied, 'there is a new owner in Dunbawn Castle.'

'That is the castle,' said the mother, 'where the rich widow lived. She pined away after the death of her beautiful daughter Maeve.'

'Yes,' said Ana. 'The new owner is the widow's nephew. He is the last of the family and will inherit all the wealth.'

'What is his name?' asked Gobnait.

'Brian is his name. He is a fine, handsome young man.'

'And who will live with him in the Castle?' asked Mella.

'Oh! there are many attendants, but the principal one is Nuala, his old nurse. She has been with him since he was born. Both his parents have been dead for some years. I must be going now, for I have some distance to walk to the next house.'

'Oh, Ana, don't go till you tell me my fortune,' said Mella.

'And mine,' said Gobnait and Roisin, speaking together.

'Now, girls, I cannot tell you your fortune, but I can tell you how to get good luck for yourselves. I am doing this for your sake, Roisin.'

The three girls gathered round her, anxiously waiting to hear what she would say.

'Your face is your fortune, *asthore*,' she said to Roisin, 'but it is your kind heart that will bring you the good luck.'

Ana smiled as she said:

'Now listen, girls.

'You all know the high bank at the back of the strand near the Black Rock.'

'Yes,' came in a chorus.

'If you climb the bank you will come to a field. Walk through the field to the stone fence at the end.'

'Is it a long field?' asked lazy Gobnait.

'Yes, and when you have crossed the fence you will come to another field, a larger one.'

'Must we walk through that too?' asked Mella.

'Yes. And when you have crossed the fence at the far end you must walk through another field, much larger than either of the others.'

'Oh! I could never do that,' said Gobnait.

'Well, if you could not, it is useless for me to tell you any more.'

'Oh, go on, Ana,' said Mella. 'Don't mind lazy Gobnait.'

'Yes, go on,' said Gobnait, 'perhaps I could try the long walk.'

Ana continued:

'At the end of the third field there is a little wood. The trees form a kind of circle. In the centre of the circle there is a stone chair. This is the Wishing Chair. Anyone who sits in it can wish three times. In this way they can get three things which they desire.'

'I'll start off in the morning,' said Gobnait.

'No,' said Ana. 'You must go in the order of age. Mella first, then Gobnait and then Roisin. I must leave you now. I wish you all good luck. Good night.'

'I'll get up at cock crow in the morning,' said Mella.

'You will,' laughed Gobnait, 'if the cock begins to crow at midday. That is your usual time for rising.'

'You are not such an early riser yourself,' was the angry retort from Mella. Turning to Roisin, she said: 'You call me when you yourself are getting up.'

Next morning Mella left the house at an early hour. She walked briskly to the sea shore. When she reached the high banks she thought she would hardly be able to climb to the top of them. She made a great effort but by the time she had crossed the third field she was exhausted and parched with thirst.

With lagging steps, she came to the little wood. As she sat down in the chair she forgot everything but her desire for a drink. She cried aloud, 'Oh, how I wish I had a drink of clear, cold water.' Immediately the leaves on the trees overhead seemed to sing the words, 'Your wish will be granted.'

There at her feet she saw a well of sparkling water and a vessel at the brink.

She took a long drink and then remembered that one of her wishes was gone.

'My second wish is that I will have roses in my cheeks like the lovely colour that Roisin has in hers.'

Again the leaves seemed to sing—

'Your wish will be granted.'

All at once nice pink roses appeared in her cheeks, but there were thorns in each which pricked her.

'Oh!' she cried, 'my third wish is that these thorny

roses will go away. Bad as my yellow face was it did not hurt like this.'

The voices in the leaves answered—

'Your wish will be granted.'

The water in the well turned yellow and in it she saw her face reflected.

'You don't look very happy,' said Gobnait as her sister reached home, weary and footsore.

'Never mind how I look,' snapped Mella.

'Well,' said Gobnait, 'I will try my luck tomorrow and I hope I will come home happier than you are after your adventure.'

Next morning, Gobnait rose early. She ate a good substantial breakfast, for she had always a great appetite.

Her experience was much the same as her sister's till she reached the wishing chair.

The fresh air made her very hungry.

'I'm starving,' she cried out.

'I wish I had a good dinner.'

The voices in the leaves called out—

'Your wish will be granted.'

There beside her, on a crystal tray, she saw a delicious meal. She ate heartily. Then she remembered that one of her wishes was gone.

'My second wish is that I will have a nice slight figure instead of being so fat and bulky.'

The voices in the leaves said –

'Your wish will be granted.'

Thereupon she felt her body shrinking and shrinking till her clothes hung so loosely round her that she looked like a long pole. Her feet seemed now to be enormous under her thin, lean body.

'Oh,' she said, 'I wish I had my own figure back again.'

Again came the song in the leaves —

'Your wish will be granted.'

All at once her own appearance returned.

She went home and ate a fine supper. Then she went to bed and tried to sleep off her disappointment.

On the third morning, Roisin got up very early. She left everything in order for the three lazy women who were still sleeping.

After a hasty meal she set out for the Wishing Chair.

The beauty of the morning made her glad. The sea was calm and sparkling under the golden rays of the sun. As she went through the fields she stopped for a moment to gather some of the wild scabious that grew on the borders of the fields. All was calm and peaceful in the brightness of the lovely summer day.

Still it was a weary girl that reached the Wishing Chair. She sat down on the chair, worn out for want of food and rest.

Unconsciously she called out —

'I wish I could rest and slumber a while.'

The voices in the leaves sang —

'Your wish will be granted.'

Suddenly she was asleep and dreaming. In her dream she saw a tall, handsome man. He smiled at her and seemed about to speak. While still half-dreaming, she exclaimed –

'Oh! how I wish that such a man as that would be my husband.'

The voices in the leaves sang –

'Your wish will be granted.'

'My third wish is that I will soon have a home far away from my aunt and cousins.'

The voices in the leaves answered –

'Your wish will be granted.'

She began her return journey. After having walked about a mile she heard a cry from a small tree by the wayside. As she stopped she saw a bird hanging from one of the branches. A thread or hair had evidently got entangled in its foot. She climbed up the bank where the tree grew and set the captive free.

The bird flew to a neighbouring tree. It chirrupped gaily, as if to thank the friend who had given it its liberty.

As Roisin was descending from the bank she came upon a large stone and hurt her foot badly. When she tried to walk she found she could not move without severe pain.

Her home was far distant and very few people came along the way. To add to her troubles her dress had got badly torn.

Poor Roisin was in despair. She sat down by the wayside and cried. After a while she heard the sound of

Suddenly she was asleep and dreaming

approaching footsteps. Round a bend in the road a woman came into sight. To her relief and delight she saw her friend Ana Criona coming towards her.

'What is the matter with my *cailin dilis* (my dear girl)?' were Ana's first words.

While Roisin was telling her friend all that had happened, a sound of wheels was heard. Round the curve came a splendid carriage drawn by two fine horses.

Ana rushed forward and stood in front of the carriage. It stopped. The door was opened by the footman. A young man alighted. Roisin looked at his face and uttered a cry. She would have fallen if Ana had not caught her as she became unconscious.

The stranger was the man she had seen in her dream.

Ana recognized him as Brian, the new owner of Dunbawn Castle.

'Oh! Sir,' said Ana, 'have pity on this poor girl. She has hurt her foot and is not able to walk.'

'Where is her home?' Brian asked.

'A good distance from here, if indeed, it can be called a home for there will be small comfort when she goes there.'

Roisin had now partly recovered consciousness.

'Will you come with her if I take her to my home?' asked Brian.

'Gladly will I go. I would do anything for the girl I love so well.'

Turning to Roisin she said —

'Come now, my girl, good fortune has sent a carriage

to bring you to a nicer place than the home you have left.'

Still in a half-swoon, Roisin was helped into the carriage. Ana sat beside her and talked cheerfully, telling her all would be well.

The carriage stopped outside a splendid castle. When the door was opened an elderly woman with a kindly face came forward to meet Brian.

'I have brought visitors, Nuala,' he said.

Roisin, half dazed with wondering, was led to the door.

'Well, my son,' said Nuala, 'if kindness and beauty are recommendations, the visitors have certainly a big share of both.'

She led them to a fine room and placed Roisin on a comfortable couch.

Brian came into the room and soon Nuala had heard the whole history of the meeting.

'I must go to some friends I promised to see this evening,' said Brian. 'I will not be back for some days. Will you, Nuala, take care of our guests till I return?'

'That I will do and welcome,' said Nuala. 'Indeed it will be nice to have someone young in the house.'

Soon Roisin was in a comfortable room with a dainty meal placed before her. Ana shared the meal and cheered the patient with the interesting things she had to tell her.

'Now, Roisin,' said Nuala, 'rest for a while. Ana and I will have a little chat.'

When the two women were talking together, Nuala said —

'I have taken Roisin to my heart. Her beautiful fair hair and blue eyes remind me of my dear boy's cousin Maeve. I will be lonely when she leaves.'

A far-away look came into Ana's eyes as she said, 'Yes, when she leaves.'

Gradually the sprained foot improved until Roisin was able to walk without trouble.

'Now, Ana,' she said, 'since I am able to walk again I should return home. I fear I have outstayed my welcome by remaining so long.'

'Oh, *alanna*,' said Nuala, 'don't think of going until my dear boy comes back. He would never forgive me if I let you go without seeing him again. What do you say, Ana?'

Ana paused and looked very wise. Then she said, 'My advice is that Roisin stays.'

There was now the question of dress to be considered as Roisin's own had been so badly torn.

'Will the pair of you come with me to Maeve's room?' asked Nuala.

'There are many dresses there which the poor girl never wore.'

Ana was lost in admiration of Roisin when she saw her arrayed in a magnificent dress.

'I always knew you were beautiful,' she said, 'but you now look like some wonderful creature from fairyland.'

'Perhaps,' said Nuala, 'you would like to see the different rooms in the house.'

'Oh, yes,' was the answer from both.

'Here,' said Nuala, 'is the room where poor Maeve used to play the harp.'

'Oh, may I play, please?' asked Roisin.

'Of course, *asthore*, and welcome. Come, Ana, and I will show the other rooms.'

Roisin forgot everything in her delight in the music. She played on and on and did not notice that the door of the room had been opened until she heard a voice say, 'Maeve.' She turned round and saw Brian standing in the room.

'I fear I have startled you,' he said. 'For a moment I thought my cousin Maeve was back again. Please continue to play.'

Roisin was unable to play. She felt as if she were again in the Wishing Chair dreaming of the handsome young man who now stood by her side.

Ana and Nuala came into the room. 'Now,' said Ana, 'I can start on my travels again. The roving life suits me best.'

'I wish you would stay, Ana,' said Brian, 'but I understand your longing to return to your old way of life, but I want to ask you to leave Roisin with us.'

'Oh, yes, Ana,' said Nuala, 'please leave Roisin with us.'

'Won't you stay, Roisin?' asked Brian, 'And stay always, for from the moment I first saw you I knew you were the girl I would like to make my wife.'

'And perhaps later on,' said Ana, with a knowing smile, 'she will tell you of the first moment she saw you.'

Nuala took Roisin in her arms, saying – 'Oh, we will now have a happy home. My dear boy won't be lonely any more.'

'But my aunt and cousins!' said Roisin.

'Your aunt and cousins!' exclaimed Ana. 'If ever they attempt to come near you I'll get all the bad fairies in the country to plague them day and night. *Slan agaibh* (good bye) now. My next visit will be for the happy wedding.' With these words she hurried off.

The wedding was one of the grandest ever seen in the countryside and Brian and Roisin lived happy ever after.

The Magic Gifts

Once upon a time, and a very good time it was, there was a poor widow who had a son named Jack. Jack was a good boy, but he was very simple and had not much sense. The mother found it hard to get food and the other necessaries of life for herself and her son. So Jack at last made up his mind to go and seek his fortune.

After walking for miles and miles he came to a farmer's house. The farmer and his wife made him welcome and gave him a good supper. When he had eaten enough they all sat around the fire and talked. Jack was astonished and shocked to hear the farmer and his family boasting of the way they had cheated and tricked their neighbours, but when he went to bed he thought no more about it.

Early next morning he left the house, and the farmer's wife gave him a griddle cake to eat on his journey. Towards evening he came to a large green. In the centre of the green there was a huge clump of furze covering a rock.

As he came nearer Jack was surprised to see that the rock was scooped out so as to make a neat little dwelling-house. The front of the house was whitewashed and the thatched roof looked as if it had been freshly put on. A nice old woman was leaning over the half-door. Jack wished her good evening. The woman, smiling kindly, returned his greeting and asked if he would like to rest for the night at her house. 'You must be tired after walking all day,' she said.

Jack said he would be delighted, and after he had a good supper the woman told him that if he wished he could remain in the house and help to mind the cows and goats and hens and to keep the bit of land in order.

He agreed to this. He worked well, and the woman was very kind to him. After three months had gone by she suggested that he should go home to see his mother. The old woman said he could return to her house whenever he wished.

Jack was pleased with this arrangement and when he was leaving the old woman gave him a hen, which she said would serve as wages for his work.

'Bring the bird to your mother,' she said, 'put it on the table and give it some oats. Then say: "Hen, hen, lay your eggs," and you'll see something that will surprise you.'

Jack thanked the woman and went off with the hen. He came to the house where he had stayed before and they gave him a great welcome and invited him to spend the night there.

After he had eaten his supper, Jack and the family sat around the fire and talked.

'How did you get on since you were here before?' they asked him.

Then Jack told them of his work and how the old woman had given him a hen for his wage.

'However,' he added, 'maybe it's a good bargain, because she told me that if I put it on the table and gave it some oats and said: "Hen, hen, lay your eggs," then I would get a great surprise.'

'Let's do it now and see what happens,' said the farmer's wife.

'All right,' said Jack and he went out and got the hen and put her on the table.

The farmer's wife gave her some oats and Jack said: 'Hen, hen, lay your eggs.'

The hen picked at the oats and at the same time she began to lay golden eggs as fast as one could count them. By the time she had finished the oats she had laid about twenty.

The people of the house were delighted and so was Jack. They gave him a lovely bed in the best room and made a nest for the hen beside the bed.

Next morning he set out for home, taking with him the hen and a big griddle cake which the woman of the house had made for him.

His mother was filled with joy to see her son again. After he had told her about his travels, he showed her what he said was the most wonderful hen in Eirinn.

'She looks just like any other hen,' said his mother.

'Put some oats on the table and you'll see, mother,' he said.

She did as he told her and then he put the hen on the table beside the oats and said: 'Hen, hen, lay your eggs.' But the hen went on picking and not an egg did she lay.

'Oh! my poor foolish boy,' said the mother, 'you had no sense when you left home and you have less now.'

'I have been cheated, mother,' said Jack, 'but I will try my fortune again,' and then he told her about the hen that laid the golden eggs.

'That farmer and his family cheated you indeed,' said his mother. 'Tomorrow morning go off to the old woman again and tell her what has happened.'

He went off again and arrived at the farmer's house. He told them that the hen would not lay any golden eggs for him. They laughed and pretended they had never seen the hen that laid the golden eggs and that Jack had only dreamt all that nonsense. Poor Jack did not know what to think, and when he returned to the old woman he told her all that had happened.

'You were foolish, Jack,' she said, 'to try to find out what the hen could do till you went home. The hen you brought to your mother was not the one I gave you.'

'I wonder,' said Jack, 'would the kind people who gave me such a welcome do such a mean thing as to steal the hen.'

'You can't help it now. Go back to your work of minding the animals,' said the old woman.

The cows and all the other animals were glad to have Jack back, for he was very kind to them. After a week, the old woman told him to go home again to see his mother.

'Here is a tablecloth,' she said, 'but do not open it till you reach your own home. Then spread it on the table and say: "Tablecloth, do your duty."'

Jack set out again next day and soon he came to the farmer's house. He kept the tablecloth round his body so that the people of the house would not see it. They made jokes about what they called his dream and asked him what wages he had got this time.

Jack would not tell them, but at last one of the children peeped under his coat and saw the cloth. They teased him and laughed at him so much that in the end he spread the cloth on the table and, forgetting the old woman's warning, said:

'Tablecloth, do your duty.'

In a moment it was covered with golden plates, jugs, tumblers, knives and forks. The dishes contained delicious foods and the jugs and tumblers were filled with the richest wine. Everyone had a most delightful meal and when it was over Jack gave all the golden utensils to the woman of the house.

That night he was given the same fine bed as he had slept in on the other night, and the farmer's wife put the tablecloth under his pillow.

Next morning he got up early and, taking the tablecloth from under his pillow, he set out for home. When he got there he took out the tablecloth and showed it to his mother. However, when he put the cloth on the table he was very disappointed to find that neither golden vessels nor fine food appeared. His mother laughed at him for being so foolish, but he determined to go again to the house under the furze bush.

On his way back he stayed with the farmer's family. They laughed at him when he spoke of the tablecloth.

'It was another dream you had, Jack,' said they, 'a dream like the one you had about the hen.'

When Jack came to the old woman's house and told her all that had happened she told him she had only one gift left.

'Take this stick,' she said, 'and whenever you say: "Stick, do your duty," you will see something that will surprise you, but be careful, for this is the last present I will give you.' Jack thanked her and set out for home once more.

On his way home he stayed at the farmer's house again. Jack did not hide his gift this time and the people of the house talked a good deal about it.

At last Jack said: 'Well, as I showed you what the hen could do and what the tablecloth could do, or, as you say, what I dreamt they could do, I will show you what the stick can do, but first let me warn you it may all be a dream.'

'I think it is,' said the farmer's wife with a smile.

The stick went on beating harder than ever

'Now,' said he, 'stick, do your duty.'

On the moment the stick flew from one to another of the whole household, whacking and beating every member, until there were shouts of pain and panic from every side. It moved like lightning and just as a person would be rising from a blow, back came the stick to give him another thrashing.

'Oh! Jack,' said the woman of the house, 'stop the stick and we will give you back your hen.'

'But you said, my good woman, that the hen was only a dream,' said Jack.

'Oh, here she is for you, Jack, and stop the stick,' she said and she opened a door and there sat Jack's hen.

'Stick, stick, will that do?' said Jack, but the stick went on beating harder than ever.

'Oh! Jack,' said the woman, 'here is your tablecloth,' and, opening a drawer, she took out the cloth and gave it to him.

'Stick, stick, stop now,' said Jack. The stick flew back to Jack's hand, but the farmer and his family continued moaning with pain for a long time as they rubbed their aching limbs.

Jack would not stay a moment longer among such deceitful people. He slept in an out-house and reached home in the evening. His mother's joy knew no bounds when she saw the wonderful hen and the magic cloth.

She and Jack lived very happily together, and because of the magic gifts, they never saw a poor day again.

However, they spent their money wisely and were very good to the poor.

One day they drove in a carriage to the place where the old fairy woman had lived. The furze and the rock were there, but the house had disappeared. There was no trace of cows or sheep or the other animals. All was silent and still, and Jack never saw his kind old friend again.

The Verdant Valley

Oh! 'tis sweet to fancy that among the flowers,
Fairy voices murmur sweeter strains than ours.
(Old Song)

'Well, Aoife, all our sons and daughters, except Donal, have gone from us now.'

'Yes, indeed, Fionn, and I suppose we will not long have him with us. I wonder he has not already chosen a wife.'

'I hope when he does choose one he will be as happy as all the other members of the family are in their married life.'

'We ourselves will be a bit lonely when our youngest child leaves us,' said Fionn.

'Yes,' Aoife replied. 'The children go from us just as the young birds leave the nest.'

'True, Aoife, but I wish Donal would marry while we are still living. Life would be lonely for him if we were gone.'

The speakers were a rich man named Fionn and his wife, Aoife. They were sitting by a blazing fire in one of the large rooms of their stately mansion. It was mid-winter and snow was falling heavily.

Just then Donal passed by a window. He waited to remove his cloak and strong shoes before entering the room where his parents were. He was tall and handsome, kindly and thoughtful and, as his mother said of him, 'a dreamer of dreams'.

'We have been speaking about you, Donal,' said the mother as he came into the room.

'Well, my dear parents, I suppose you have been discussing the usual question as to how soon I will think of taking a wife.'

'I confess, Donal, something of that nature has been in our minds,' said the mother.

'And in your words too, Mother. Well, that is not altogether remarkable for my own thoughts have been running in the same direction.'

'What gave rise to such thoughts?' the father asked.

'I was looking at the falling snow. It seemed to form a white carpet over the fields and roads. Near the house here a crow lighted on a holly tree. A strange thought came into my mind. I know it will seem an odd one to both of you.'

'What was it?' asked the mother.

'The white snow, the black plumage of the bird and the red berries of the holly suggested the thought that I would like to marry a girl who had beautiful black hair, clear white skin and rosy lips.'

'Well, my boy,' said the father, 'perhaps you will yet meet such a girl as that but during my long travels I have never met one who completely answers that description.'

'Speaking of travels, father, I have been thinking of visiting the Verdant Valley.'

'Surely not at this time of the year,' said the mother.

'Yes. This is the time when the valley is at its best. The yew trees, holly and all the evergreens stand out in beauty under the sombre winter sky.'

'You know there is a fine castle in the valley,' said the father.

'Yes. Who lives there now?'

'It is generally believed that the present inmates are not the rightful owners.'

'I have never heard that,' said Donal.

'Well, here is the story your mother and I have been told. The former owner was a widower named Oscar. He had one child. Etain was her name. Some time after his first wife's death, he married a widow called Nessa. She, too, had a daughter. Her name was Grania. It was said the name suited her for she was very ugly. The girls were about the same age. Grania was jealous of Etain because of her beauty but neither she nor her mother showed any sign of envy or dislike while Oscar was present.

'A sad day came for poor Etain. A short time ago her father died. Immediately after his death Nessa took possession of the castle. Then Etain disappeared. It was said she had gone to live with some relatives whose home was a great distance from the castle.'

'Has she never been seen in the valley since her father's death?' asked Donal.

'No, never, and no one in the neighbourhood knows where she is.'

'And,' said Aoife, 'many believe that Nessa and Grania have banished the poor girl and that she may be in some place where she is lonely and unhappy.'

'It seems a strange thing, Mother, that the girl should disappear like that. Well, I will go to the Verdant Valley and feast my eyes on the beauty of which I have heard so much.'

'Will you go alone?' asked the mother.

'Yes. I wish to have the pleasure of seeing and re-membering the charm of the valley and I can have this more fully if I am alone.'

'Well now, my son, before you begin your journey I would like to give you a word of advice. The fairies have their homes near the roads which lead to the valley. Remember if you meet them be gentle and friendly. They can be either helpful friends or bitter foes.'

Next morning, Donal set out on his journey. His mother made sure that he was warmly clad. He had travelled some distance when he came to a little house by the wayside. From within came cries like those of an animal in pain. An old woman appeared at the door.

'Oh! kind stranger,' she said. 'I heard your footsteps. I wonder could you come to my aid.'

'I shall be glad to help you in any way I can,' was

Donal's reply. When he entered the house he saw the cause of the shrieks.

'Look,' said the woman, 'there is my poor dog in great pain. There is a big thorn in one of his front paws and my sight is so bad I cannot get it out.'

Donal removed the thorn as gently as possible. The grateful animal frisked about him in delight to have been relieved from the pain. Not less were the joy and gratitude of the woman.

'Oh! how I wish I could do something to reward you for this great, kind deed,' she said.

'I am richly rewarded by being able to give you such joy and to relieve the poor dog from the pain.'

'May I ask why you are travelling in such severe weather?'

'I am well clad and well prepared for the cold. My reason for travelling at this time is that I want to see the Verdant Valley in its winter beauty.'

'So you are going to the Verdant Valley.'

'Yes, and I shall be pleased to receive any advice you can give me.'

'On your way to the Valley you will meet some of "the good people".'

'You mean the fairies.'

'Yes. Now be gentle and kind with them and be sure to do as they ask. They can be great, helpful friends but they can also be hard, revengeful enemies. Now start on your journey and my blessing goes with you.'

Donal had travelled some miles when he saw a little man standing by a small lake. He was looking down at the water. He spoke –

That stone which in the water lies
I fain would have and greatly prize
If you procure that stone for me
A kindly act I'll do for thee.

The lake was shallow and Donal had no difficulty in getting the stone.

'Now,' said the little man, 'take this stone. It has the power of giving off rays of light that will make visible any objects placed before it. The light will penetrate through all things, glass, wood or even stone. Remember, however, this stone can be used once only. May it bring you good luck. Farewell!'

Donal thanked the fairy and continued his journey. He had travelled some miles when he saw another little man. This one was sitting under a yew tree. He spoke these words –

In a hole beneath that tree
You will find a magic key
Which will unlock the strongest door
From cellar low to topmost floor.

The hole was deep but Donal succeeded in getting the key.

'Now,' said the little man, 'this key may be of service to you but it can be used once only.'

Donal thanked the man and proceeded on his way. He walked on till he saw a third little man sitting near the top of a hillock. At the foot lay a small, brightly coloured scarf. The little man spoke –

Oh! stranger passing on the way
Restore that scarf to me I pray
And for this simple, kindly deed
Success and joy will be your meed.

Donal handed the scarf to the fairy, who said: 'Anyone who puts on this scarf will have, while wearing it, the strength of ten men. Remember, however, that the strength remains only while the wearer is performing one feat. After the feat is completed the scarf disappears.'

Donal thanked the fairy and resumed his journey.

At last he reached the Verdant Valley. He stood still gazing at its beauty. 'It well deserves its name,' he thought as he looked at the yew trees, holly and numerous evergreens. Just then Nessa and Grania came out of the castle.

'Mother,' whispered Grania, 'who is the handsome stranger?'

'Hush, child. I know him. He is the son of the rich chieftain, Fionn.'

'Welcome to the Valley,' said both as they went forward to meet him. Donal thanked them for their greeting.

'I had heard so much of the beauty of the Valley,' he said, 'I have made the journey to see it for myself.'

'I am sure you must be weary after your long journey,'

said Nessa. 'Won't you come into the castle and rest?'

Donal could not refuse the invitation without seeming ungracious. Both mother and daughter did all in their power to entertain their guest and make him welcome.

'I hope you will remain with us for some time,' said Nessa.

'I fear I cannot stay long. My parents expect me to return soon.'

'Well,' said Grania, 'you will at least give us the pleasure of your company for a few days.'

'Thank you very much for your kind hospitality but I must return tomorrow.'

When all in the castle were fast asleep Donal went out in the grounds to view the beauty of the moonlit valley. As he walked round he caught sight of a great, high tower at the back of the castle. A winding stair led to a door near the top. At a little distance from the door was a window which was so black that neither sunlight nor moonlight could penetrate the darkness. Suddenly, Donal heard hurrying footsteps. He looked round and saw an elderly man close behind him.

'Oh! kind sir,' said the man, 'I feared I would have no opportunity of speaking to you.'

'Why do you wish to speak to me?' asked Donal.

'Are you not the son of the chieftain, Fionn?'

'Yes. Who are you that seems to know my father?'

'I knew the chieftain, Fionn, when I was a boy. My name is Fiachra!'

'Oh! I have heard my father speak of you.'

'Now I ask you to listen to what I have to say. I came to this house when my late master was a young man. When he died I remained here for the sake of Etain, his daughter.'

'Where is Etain now?'

'In prison in that tower. The wicked women Nessa and Grania took possession of the castle. They wished to get Etain out of the way, but they were afraid to kill her. They sent out word that she had gone to live with some relations who live a long way from here but the truth is that they imprisoned her in that tower. No one but me knows where she is and I myself would not know only that on the morning after she disappeared I found her pearl necklace near the tower. Then I thought I heard sobs and moans from inside the tower but I was powerless to free her.'

'She will die if she remains there,' said Donal.

'Nessa and Grania bring food to her, not indeed in kindness but that they fear their villainy might be found out if she died.'

'Wait here a while till I return,' said Donal.

It seemed but a moment till he came back with the three gifts the fairies had given him. He held the stone up towards the window in the tower. Immediately, the window became bright and transparent. There, gazing through it was a lovely girl. The stone fell from Donal's hand and disappeared. He stood still in wonder. Etain's

'But how can we reach her?' asked Fiachra

black hair, beautiful skin and rosy lips completed the picture he had seen in his day dreams.

'But how can we reach her?' asked Fiachra. 'The ugly pair have the only key which unlocks the door of the tower.'

Donal climbed the steps that led to the top of the tower. After one turn of the fairy key the door flew open. The key disappeared. The sudden noise so startled Etain that she fell on the floor in a faint. The third of the fairy gifts now came into use. Donal placed the scarf round his neck. His strength became so great that he carried the unconscious girl down to the foot of the steps with ease. In surprise and disappointment he saw that Fiachra was not there. In a moment, however, he appeared.

'I have got the best carriage and two of the swiftest horses to take us away,' he said.

Donal carried the still unconscious girl to the carriage. As he reached it she revived from the swoon. The scarf vanished.

'Oh! where am I?' asked Etain. Then she saw Fiachra.

'Oh! my dear, faithful friend, tell me what has happened.'

'We must make haste and depart and then I will tell you all.'

When Etain heard of the way she had been rescued she was so grateful and happy that she could hardly speak her thanks.

'Where are we going now?' she asked.

'To my parents' home,' Donal replied. When they reached Donal's home a warm welcome was given to all three.

'Now, my dear girl,' said Aoife, 'you must take a thorough rest. Later on we can talk over things and arrange matters for a happy future.'

There was consternation in the minds of the wicked pair when they discovered that Etain had escaped.

'Let the swiftest horses be yoked at once,' ordered Nessa. 'We can at least have the satisfaction of knowing where the girl has gone.'

'The swiftest horses are gone,' said the coachman.

'Then yoke others so that we can set out at once.'

Soon the carriage was tearing along the road at a furious pace. A fast-flowing river ran by the side of the road on which they were travelling. Suddenly another carriage going at great speed came out from a side road. There was a head-on collision. Nessa was hurled into the rushing river. Grania, in falling, struck a big stone and was killed immediately.

When the news of the deaths was noised abroad there was little regret for the wicked pair.

Meanwhile, in Donal's home a warm welcome was given to the girl who had suffered so much. Aoife received her as if she were her own child. As the days went by it was evident that Donal had found the girl he would choose for a wife.

'You remember, Father,' he said, 'you believed it

would be hard to find the girl I would wish to marry. Well, don't you think Etain has all the qualities I desired?'

'Indeed I do, Donal. May you both live a long and happy life.'

There was a splendid wedding. Fiachra was amongst the most honoured guests.

Donal, Etain and their children lived long and happily in the Verdant Valley.

The Furze Witch

Once upon a time there lived in the western part of Ireland a king named Flan. His wife died when his daughter Lelia was very young.

Lelia grew up to be a beautiful girl. She was the pride of her father's heart, and his constant companion.

The great delight of both father and daughter was to ride through the country on their fine horses.

The king's favourite horse was named Duveen, from his black colour. Lelia named her horse Lunasa. It had been given to her on the first day of August (*Lunasa*).

One summer day Flan left home to visit a chieftain, who lived miles away.

The lovely day was succeeded by a still more beautiful night.

The moon shone brightly and the air was soft and still.

'Gormlai,' said Lelia to her old nurse, 'I will take Lunasa and go for a ride in the moonlight.'

'Do not go alone,' said Gormlai.

'I want to go alone and enjoy the beauty of the country in the moonlight.'

'I wish, *asthore*,' said Gormlai, 'you would take someone with you.'

'Oh!' laughed Lelia, 'you are afraid I might meet *bean draoi an aitinn* (the witch of the furze).

'Did you ever see her, Gormlai?'

'No, indeed, and from all I have heard of her I hope I never will. I believe her hut is underground in the furze field at the back of the furze hedge.'

'I know the furze hedge and the lovely little river that flows beside it. Some people say that the witch can be good as well as wicked. I heard that, if one speaks kindly to her, she might be helpful in time of trouble.'

'Well, *alanna*, no matter what sort she is, I would advise you to keep out of her way.'

Lunasa seemed to fly along the roads and through the fields. It was as if he wished to give all possible pleasure to the rider, whom he so much loved.

Lelia let him go as he willed. After some time he came to a running stream. There was a thick furze hedge all along the far side. Lelia knew she was near the witch's home.

She stopped the horse and dismounted.

From behind the hedge a strange, harsh voice called out:

'I am in great pain. Come to my aid and rich will be your reward.'

'I cannot cross the stream,' said Lelia, 'and, even if I could, the furze hedge is too thick and prickly for me to pass through.'

The voice answered.

'Lead your horse along the stream in the direction in

Lelia gave the drink to the witch

which it flows. You will come to stepping stones. At this place there is a gap in the hedge. Cross the stones and come to me.'

Lelia led the horse along till she came to the stepping stones. She tied him to a tree and crossed over the stones. There lying on the ground she saw a strange looking old hag.

'This,' she thought, 'is the witch of the furze field.'

'I fell and hurt my back,' said the witch, 'and cannot rise. Nothing will cure me but a drink from the stream.'

'But where can I find a vessel to hold the water?' asked Lelia.

'Look,' said the witch, 'by the side of the stream is a pitcher which I was about to fill.'

Lelia gave the drink to the witch.

She was immediately cured.

'For your kind act,' she said, 'I will at any time use my magic power to help you.'

'How can I find you again?' asked Lelia.

'I cannot cross the stream,' said the witch, 'but if you come in the night over the stepping stones, I will come to you.'

The witch then gave Lelia a little horn.

'If you wish to see me again, blow three times on this horn. Here, too, is a magic key which will open any lock from the weakest to the strongest.'

Having said these words the witch spread out her cloak and seemed to fly away.

Next day Lelia waited eagerly for her father's return. As the hours went by she became anxious.

Alas! Not without cause. At night time two messengers arrived with the sad news that he would return no more.

He had always been a keen swimmer. Early in the morning he had gone into the sea alone. A man on the beach stood in amazement looking at his wonderful strokes.

Suddenly he seemed to struggle and in a little while he had disappeared.

'Oh, Gormlai,' said Lelia, 'what can have happened to my poor father?'

'You know, *achusla*, his heart has not been strong for a long time. He should not have ventured into the sea alone.'

Poor Lelia was broken-hearted.

'I have no one left to love me now,' she said, 'except you, Gormlai, and Art, your kind husband.'

'Well, you know, *asthore*, no matter what happens we will love you to the end.'

Lelia now knew she would have to leave the palace. The heir to the throne would come to rule in her father's place.

Cairbre, son of a haughty widow named Macha, was to be the new king.

By his request, Lelia was to remain in the palace till some time after the coronation. Cairbre was curious to see and know the daughter of the late king.

On the eve of the great day he went alone to the palace.

Lelia happened to be walking in the garden as he approached the gates. He gazed in admiration at her lovely dark hair and sweet, sad face.

'How beautiful she is!' he thought. 'How splendidly she would reign as queen.'

He turned away. Lelia had not seen him.

There were many handsome women present at the gorgeous spectacle of Cairbre's coronation. As he looked round he thought that Lelia was the fairest of them all.

'Mother,' he said, when all the festivities were over, 'I think I have today seen the girl who will be my queen.'

'There were many lovely women at the assembly,' the mother replied, 'but in my opinion Lelia was the most beautiful of them all.'

'Oh, Mother, I am delighted you think so. She is the one I will ask to be my wife.'

Lelia was preparing to leave the palace. Art and Gormlai were to go with her to a house at some distance away. The house had belonged to her mother.

On the day before her intended departure, Cairbre came to the room she was in. She was looking out the window, thinking sadly of bygone days.

'Lelia,' said Cairbre, 'you will not leave the palace tomorrow.'

'Why do you say that?' asked Lelia.

'You will stay here and be my wife.'

'Oh, no,' was all the girl could say.

Cairbre looked at her in surprise and anger.

'You do not wish to marry me?'

Lelia rose from her seat and looked at him steadily.

'I do not wish to marry you,' she said.

Cairbre went hastily from the room to find his mother.

If he was angry and indignant, his mother was more so. She was furious.

'Is the girl mad, refusing to be the wife of a king?' she exclaimed, 'and as well as that the greatest and noblest man in all the land?'

'What will we do, Mother?' Cairbre asked.

'What will we do? We will compel the stupid girl to marry you. She is clever and beautiful and would be a great queen. I believe she is beloved by the people. I have always given you everything you desired and I will not fail you now. Let me think of some plan to bring the silly girl to her senses.'

Later in the day Macha called her son to her.

'I have a plan,' she said. 'If Lelia still refuses to marry you, tell her you will give her three days to consider the matter. If at the end of that time she does not consent to be your wife you will have her imprisoned in one of the dungeons in the castle. There she will learn sense and gratitude.'

When Lelia heard of the terrible fate that was destined for her, she went at once to her loved nurse.

'Gormlai,' she said, 'what am I to do to escape from this cruel pair?'

'Wait, *asthore*, I have thought of a way for you to

escape. Art and I will mount Duveen and you Lunasa. We will go like the wind and reach your mother's house before the cruel king will know we have gone.'

In a very short time the horses were ready and the riders set off.

Unfortunately, Macha had been wakeful in the night. She heard the trampling of the horses and at once gave the alarm.

Cairbre called together a number of his attendants and started off in pursuit.

Lelia and her friends had not gone far when they heard the sound of the galloping horses.

Looking round they saw they were close behind them.

'Gormlai,' said Lelia, 'Cairbre will take me back with him.'

'I fear he will, *asthore*.'

'Will you, Gormlai, and Art, take care of the two horses and continue your journey. The animals will be safe and well cared for by you.'

Cairbre and his men had now reached the poor fugitives.

'Halt!' said he in a voice of thunder.

Turning to his men, he said:

'Use your swords if necessary. Take the girl and let the others follow their own course.'

Art and Gormlai knew it would be futile to offer any resistance. They rode away.

In the midst of her trouble Lelia was consoled by the thought that the horses would be well cared for.

'Now Lelia,' said Cairbre when they reached the palace, 'I have said I would give you three days in which to decide whether you will become my wife or be imprisoned in the dark dungeon.'

'I prefer life in a dungeon to marriage with you,' was Lelia's reply.

'Well, take two days to think over the matter,' said Cairbre as he strode out of the room.

After a short time he returned and said: 'Remember, it is useless for you to try to escape a second time. Every door will be shut and the keys will be removed from the locks.'

These words reminded Lelia that the witch had given her a magic key. She determined to go to the furze field as soon as all the inmates of the castle were asleep.

When all was still, she unlocked one of the doors and hurried from the palace.

She crossed the stepping stones and blew three times on the little horn.

The dark form of the witch seemed to fly towards her.

When Lelia told her sad story, the witch said:

'I can help you, but you must follow my instructions carefully. Wait here a moment.' She disappeared but returned in a very short time.

'Take these,' she said as she handed Lelia a pair of strange looking shoes. 'You can wear them over your own shoes. They are made from bats' wings. You can walk in them without making the least noise. They will bring you over the ground as quickly as if you were flying. In a very short time you will be far away from the palace.'

'But where will I go?' asked Lelia.

'Take the road that leads westwards. Pass every house till you come to a beautiful castle. Go to the kitchen quarters and ask for food and a place to rest.

'You are sure to be received with kind hospitality. Next morning ask leave to stay in the castle as a worker in the kitchen. You must not wear your own fine clothes. Dress as a working girl.'

'I can manage to do that,' said Lelia. 'Gormlai, my old nurse, has left some of her worn clothes in her room.'

'One word more,' said the witch. 'On no account tell who you are. Let that be found out in its own time. Now hurry back. When all is quiet and still in the palace tomorrow night, steal out and away.'

The witch vanished without waiting for a word of thanks.

Lelia put on the magic shoes.

In what seemed but a moment of time she reached the castle.

In Gormlai's room she found the clothes necessary for the disguise.

It was grief to her to part with her lovely dresses and jewels.

'One treasure I must take with me,' she thought.

This was a *mionn oir* (golden diadem) which her father had given to her mother on their wedding day.

She fastened the ornament under her dress and hurried

away. Such was the power of the magic shoes that she was a great distance from the palace before it was known that she was gone.

When the king heard she had escaped, he gave orders that followers should be sent in all directions.

He himself was foremost amongst them. In urging his horse to leap over a fast flowing river he was thrown and carried away in the rushing waters.

His death was such a shock to his mother she did not long survive him.

When Lelia reached the castle the magic shoes fell from her feet and disappeared completely.

She knocked at one of the lower doors. It was opened by a big, fat woman with a kindly face.

'May I rest here for the night?' Lelia asked.

'Of course you can, *alanna*. Our good lady always tells us to have a *caoin failte* (kind welcome) for all who come our way.'

Mor, as the woman was called, led Lelia into the big kitchen. She gave her a good meal and showed her a comfortable bed.

Lelia was careful to put the diadem under her pillow before settling to sleep. Next morning she fastened it securely under her dress.

When she went into the kitchen, Mor greeted her with a beaming smile.

'Your lovely face will be a delight to me,' she said.

'But,' said Lelia, 'I want to be useful. Please tell me how I can help with the work.'

'Well, go out to the garden at the side of the house and gather some fruit.'

When Lelia went out, she noticed that the road led down to the sea. Just then she saw a small carriage approaching.

Suddenly, beside the place where she stood, a fox jumped over the hedge. It was followed by a great hound. The oncoming horse started and dashed along. Lelia noticed that the reins had fallen from the driver's hands. Her knowledge of horses came to her aid. She darted and, running for a second beside the carriage, managed to grasp the reins and stop the excited horse.

The driver was none other than Oscar, the son of Conor and Ita, who were the owners of the castle.

When he had quieted the horse, he turned to Lelia and said:

'How can I thank you? But for your prompt and brave action I, with my horse, would be deep in the sea.'

Mor came out from the house. Lelia slipped quietly away.

'Mor, who is that girl?' asked Oscar.

'I do not know. She came here last night and said she would work in the kitchen if I let her stay.'

'Work in the kitchen with those delicate white hands!' exclaimed Oscar. 'Well, be kind to her, Mor. She saved my life.'

Oscar was an only child and was much loved by both of his parents.

He had a very special affection for his mother and had

no secrets from her. After his experience of the morning he sought her out to tell of his adventure.

'I am sure, Mother,' he said, 'the girl is of noble birth.'

'Well, Oscar,' replied the mother, 'don't think too much about her. You know your father is having a great ball. All the noble ladies from far and near are to be invited. He hopes you will choose a wife from among them.'

A day or two before the time arranged for the ball, Ita and Oscar were sitting at an open window which overlooked a small wood.

After a time Lelia came into the wood and sat down under a tree. Thinking she was free from observation, she took out the diadem which she had fastened under her dress.

'Look, Mother,' said Oscar, as he started to his feet 'there is the girl who saved my life.'

Ita looked more closely at Lelia. 'Oscar!' she exclaimed, 'she is the image of the dearest friend I ever had; the same beautiful dark eyes and hair. She was named Lelia. She died many years ago.'

'Come with me at once, Mother, and speak to her.'

When mother and son entered the garden, Lelia sprang to her feet. As she did so the diadem fell to the ground. She stooped hastily and lifted it up.

'What is your name, fair maiden?' Ita asked.

Lelia hesitated. Then she said:

'Lelia is my name.'

'May I see the diadem?' asked Ita.

Lelia handed it to her.

When Ita looked at it she said: 'I see here the names Flan and Lelia. Were these the names of your parents?'

'Yes,' was Lelia's answer.

'Then,' said Ita, 'you are the child of my dearest friend. I was present when she received this diadem from her young husband on her wedding day.'

'Yes,' said Lelia, 'my father gave the diadem to me and told me it had been his wedding gift to my mother.'

'Come with me, child,' said Ita.

'I will have word sent to good old Mor that you are not returning to the kitchen.' Turning to Oscar, she said: 'When Lelia and I have heard and told everything, I will send for you.'

'It seems a long time to wait, Mother,' said Oscar as she and Lelia went away.

When Ita heard all Lelia had to tell her about her childhood and later life, she was determined the girl should remain with her at the castle.

'Now, Lelia,' she said with a kind, motherly smile, 'your clothes are hardly those that should be worn by a princess. We are preparing for a great ball. You must have a beautiful dress. Rest a while till I return later on.'

Ita then sent for her son to come to her.

'Oscar,' she said, 'it is your father's wish that you will choose a wife from among the many beautiful and brilliant women who will be present at the ball.'

'Mother,' said Oscar, 'I have already seen the girl whom I would like to make my wife.'

The mother smiled, a knowing smile.

'My advice to you,' she continued, 'is that, immediately after the festivities have begun, you will enter the ballroom accompanied by the girl of your choice.'

The ballroom was a scene of great splendour. The lights shone brightly 'o'er fair women and brave men'.

'But where is Oscar?' whispered Conor to his wife.

'Wait and see,' was her reply.

At that moment there was a murmur of admiration among the guests. Oscar had entered with Lelia on his arm.

Conor showed every sign of welcome and pleasure when he saw the girl Oscar had chosen.

Very soon there was a splendid wedding and, as the old story-tellers say:

They had children in basketfuls
Rocked them in cradlefuls
And if they don't live happy
    then you and I may.

The Rightful King

'Oh! listen to the cry of the *bean sí* (banshee), Thady,' said Gormlai, the faithful servant of the young prince, Fergus.

Thady was looked on as rather a simpleton but his love for the family gave him a high place in their regard.

'I wonder,' he said, as another weird wail reached their ears, 'does the poor king hear that? I am afraid he will not see the morning.'

What Thady feared was true. King Brian was nearing the end.

'No matter who may try to prevent me I am going to the King's room,' said Gormlai. 'I know Queen Sive will not want me to be at the bedside, but I will go to be with my beloved King at the last.'

'I will go too,' said Thady.

'Yes, come, Thady. He knows how much we both love him and his son.'

In the room where the dying King lay there were three watchers: Fergus, his only child, the son of his first wife, Sive his second wife, and her son Art. Art was the son of Sive's first husband. He was some years older than Fergus.

When Gormlai and Thady entered the room they were met with unfriendly glances from Sive and Art. The King's face brightened as Gormlai knelt by his bed. He looked at Fergus and then feebly raised his hand and pointed to the crown. It had by his orders been placed on a table at a little distance from the bed.

Gormlai at once understood his meaning.

'He wishes me to place the crown on the head of the prince,' she said.

Fergus knelt to receive it. The King smiled his thanks. He was unable to speak.

Even simple Thady noticed the expression on the faces of Sive and Art.

'Did you see,' he said afterwards, 'the look on the faces of the Queen and her son?'

'Indeed I did,' Gormlai replied, 'there was no kindness in that look. It showed only disappointment and bitterness.'

Just before dawn the King died. When the news of his death went abroad many people came to the palace.

Among them was Mór, the wife of a neighbouring chieftain. Her beautiful daughter, Etain, came with her. King Brian had been very fond of Etain. He had hoped to see her married to his beloved son, Fergus.

'I am glad you have come, Etain,' said Fergus.

'I have known and loved both your parents,' Etain replied.

'Your sympathy means much to me, Etain, especially now when all my loved ones are gone.'

During this conversation Mór was closely watching the young pair. When she had an opportunity of speaking alone with Etain she said—

'My dear child, I am proud of you. I can see you have won the admiration of the future king. You will be his queen.'

'Mother,' replied the girl, 'it is not because Fergus may be king that I care for him. It is for himself alone I prize his friendship.'

After the burial of Brian the next great happening at the court was the choosing of his successor. Fergus was, of course, the rightful heir. If loyalty and affection could decide the matter he would be king. Sive, however, disputed his right to the throne. She claimed that as Art was the eldest he should reign even though he was only stepson to King Brian.

There was much dissension about the matter.

At last four druids were summoned to the palace to decide the question. They were Annla, Oilliol, Crionna and Maen.

'The territory cannot be left long without a ruler,' said Annla, the chief druid.

'There must be neither doubt nor delay about the choice,' said Oilliol, 'let us at once decide to whom the crown will pass.'

The four druids went apart and talked together. No one was allowed to be present at the conference, but Gormlai hid at the back of an old chest near the door of the room. Fergus and Etain went out to walk in a wood near the palace.

Then Annla spoke.

'Let nine men stand before us, three dark-haired, three fair-haired and three red-haired.'

'Now,' said Oilliol, 'you men will draw lots and the one who will get the tablet on which there is a figure of a horn will be the man chosen for our purpose.'

The lot fell on a huge, red-haired man named Ruan.

The other eight laughed as one called out: 'Oh! Ruan of the *goile mor* (the big appetite).'

Ruan was taken aside and given a huge meal of the broth and flesh of a white bull.

'Now,' said Annla, 'I will pronounce on him the charm of truth.'

'And I the charm of sleep,' said Oilliol.

'And I the charm of dreams,' said Crionna.

'And I the charm of vision,' said Maen. 'In this vision he will describe the person and character of the rightful king and tell where and with whom he is at the time he sees him.'

After Ruan had slept for some time he screamed out –

'I see before me a young, handsome king, blue-eyed, dark-haired, noble in bearing. Behind his left ear is a small brown mole. He is at present standing near a yew tree in the wood. Beside him is she who will be his queen.'

'That is my beloved Prince Fergus,' came from a voice behind the chest. 'How often have I said that mole would bring him luck in choosing a good wife.'

So much astonished were the druids at hearing Gormlai's voice that she had passed through the doorway before they had recovered from their amazement.

The druids gave orders for the nobles to assemble. Fergus, Etain, Mór, Sive and Art came with them.

'There is no doubt as to who will be the king,' Annla declared. 'Our charms have disclosed that Fergus, son of Brian shall be placed on the throne.'

There was general rejoicing when the announcement was made. Sive, Art and a few of their followers were the only ones who did not share in it.

While preparations for the enthronement were in progress Sive was planning and plotting how to prevent Fergus from being crowned king.

She called to her an old druid named Ardán whom she had in her power.

'I want you to ensure,' she said, 'that Fergus will not be crowned king.'

'But Your Majesty, how can I do that?'

'It is for you to find a way. You must have him captured and removed from the palace.'

'Oh! by what means?'

'*You* must find the means. You dare not disobey me since that time when, for a rich reward, you disclosed some of the druidical secrets to me.'

'That was a bitterly sad day for me.'

'Well, remember now and do as I say. Go at once and plan how you will remove Fergus from the court.'

Later in the day Ardán came to Sive.

'Your Majesty,' he said, 'is it not a custom with Prince Fergus to sail his boat in the bay at eventide?'

'Yes, he rarely fails to do that.'

'I have only one of my druidical charms left. It is the charm of the wind. When Fergus goes into his boat this evening I will put the charm on the north wind so that it will blow the boat southwards before it. There is a long stretch of deep sea through which it will pass. The wind will not cease until the prince is so far away that he cannot return.'

'And being without food he will die of hunger,' said Sive.

'Yes, for his chance of reaching land is very small.'

The sun was setting in golden glory over the calm blue sea as Fergus took his place in the boat. For a short time he sailed along with a gentle motion, but Ardán, hidden behind some rocks, pronounced the charm of the wind. Immediately a strong gale arose forcing the boat southwards at terrible speed.

Darkness came on and still the wind roared. All through the night the boat rushed on. At dawn the poor prince could still see nothing but sea and sky. The wind continued to blow fiercely but at last with good effect. An island seemed to rise out of the water. The boat was

Fergus grasped the trunk of the tree and leaped ashore

blown towards it. It crashed against the rocks that formed a boundary of that part of the island.

Near where the boat struck there was a piece of land jutting out into the sea. On it grew a large tree. Fergus grasped the trunk of the tree and leaped ashore.

He walked inland. He heard voices. As he went farther he saw a herd of goats. Presently some women came along with milking vessels. They stared at him in amazement.

'I have been shipwrecked,' he said.

The women looked blankly at him. They did not understand his language. One of them disappeared. She returned accompanied by other women. Men and children followed. Fergus beckoned to one of the men to come with him to the place where the boat had stranded. It was not there. It had sunk into the deep sea.

Now, the islanders were simple, kindly folk. When they understood that the boat was lost they were full of pity for the stranger.

'Our little fishing boats could never reach a far off country,' said one of the men.

'We must give him a home here,' said a woman.

'Yes, and try to make him happy,' said another.

A pretty dark-haired child with a basket of fruit in her hand went shyly towards Fergus. She gave him the basket. He took it and thanked her with a beaming smile.

'I am sure he is hungry,' said she. 'Let us take him to the tables where our meal is ready for us.'

They led him into the centre of the island. There on large stone tables were fish, eggs, bread, honey, nuts, fruit and many vessels full of milk.

Fergus had never in all his life enjoyed a meal as much as the one then given to him.

The islanders continued their kindness and tried to make the poor exile's life as pleasant as possible.

Days passed into weeks and weeks to months. He longed to be back in his own country. His thoughts were constantly with Etain and his friends there.

As time went by it was felt that Fergus would never return. Sive now believed that nothing could keep the kingdom from Art. By deceit and flattery she at last succeeded in getting him accepted as king.

On the day of his accession a great storm broke out.

'A bad omen,' said Annla.

As time went by the fruit failed and a blight came on the crops.

'The wrong ruler is in the land,' said Oilliol.

Sickness and want prevailed.

'There is surely a usurper on the throne,' were Crionna's words.

Sive had another object in view as well as that of making Art king. She wished to marry him to the beautiful and wealthy Etain.

Etain's mother too was anxious for the marriage. She wished to see her daughter made queen.

'Etain,' she said, 'you should marry Art. You would then be queen.'

'But, Mother, you wished me to marry Fergus.'

'Yes, when I thought he would be king.'

'Oh Mother, I see it is the throne you wish me to take as a husband, not the man. I will not marry unless Fergus returns.'

'Then you will never marry,' replied her mother in angry tones.

There was one in the palace who had never given up hope that Fergus would return. This was poor Thady. Like a faithful dog he had for months watched the shore hoping to see his loved prince come back again.

'Gormlai,' said he one day, 'do you remember how the prince and I used to send messages to each other?'

'Indeed I do, Thady. Your pet bird would go and come between you and never make a mistake.'

Thady had a wonderful way with animals. He could tame a wicked sow and coax the most stubborn old ass. The birds fed from his hand.

'I am thinking now, Gormlai,' he said, 'if I tied one of the prince's rings on the pigeon and sent him over the sea he might find him.'

'I will get you the ring with the red stone,' said Gormlai. 'The prince was wearing the one with the blue stone when he went away.'

Thady tied the ring round the pigeon's neck with a thin light chain. Days went by. He waited and waited.

At last one morning Gormlai heard her name called loudly.

'Gormlai, Gormlai, look, look, the pigeon and the ring with the blue stone in it round its neck. The prince is alive! He is alive!'

'But how can we find him?'

'I saw the boat facing south when he got into it.'

'Then he must have gone in that direction,' said Gormlai.

'Yes, now there is only one boat here that can brave the currents of the deep sea.'

'I know,' said Gormlai, 'that is Art's boat.'

'Come, Gormlai, to the landing place at dusk this evening and help me to get out that boat. Bring food with you and a lantern.'

That evening Art was walking alone by the seashore. He was sad and moody. Etain would not marry him and there was little love for him among the people.

Thady and Gormlai stole out. They put the food and lantern into the boat. Gormlai hastened back to the house.

Thady had the boat ready to sail when Art heard a noise. He went towards the place and saw Thady sailing off.

'Come back, you ruffian,' he shouted.

'I will when I find my prince,' said Thady. '*Slán leat.*'

Since the coming of the pigeon Fergus had been constantly watching for a boat.

Early one morning, to his great joy he saw one approaching. He called to some of the men to go with him to the landing place. They beckoned to the occupant of the boat to come there.

A shout went up from Thady when he recognized Fergus. When the boat was moored he jumped ashore and between laughing and crying clasped Fergus in his arms.

'My prince, my prince,' he cried, 'the brave pigeon did the work. Come home with me and put the rascal off the throne.'

The islanders were grieved to part with Fergus and indeed he felt a pang in leaving them. He had learned some of their language and had helped in their work.

'I shall never forget your kindness and hospitality,' he said.

After his return home he tried as far as he could to repay their kindness. He frequently sent them many precious things that were not to be found on the island.

The sensation caused by his return can hardly be described. His keenest joy was to see Etain on the shore waiting to welcome him.

Sive and Art hurriedly went off to a distant part of the country. The crowning took place amid scenes of tumultuous delight. Even though it was mid-winter the sun shone out brightly as if nature itself shared in the universal joy.

'The rightful king is on the throne,' was the verdict of the druids.

'Etain, I shall now be able to salute you as Queen,' said Mór.

'Mother,' replied Etain, 'if Fergus were a beggar I would be equally happy with him.'

The Strange Gardener

In olden days there lived near the shores of Lough Neagh a chieftain named Feilim and his wife Macha. They had three sons. Many years after the birth of the youngest a girl was born. She was named Orla, for, even as a baby, she had lovely golden hair. Orla was very beautiful and was the idol of both her parents. Brid, her old nurse, declared she was the loveliest child in all the world.

As Orla grew to womanhood, many suitors sought her hand, but she had no desire to marry. She preferred to remain in her own happy home.

One evening Feilim and Macha were sitting at a window looking at the setting sun.

'Sometimes,' remarked Feilim, 'the sunset reminds me of the evening of life and that I have not many more years to live.'

'Oh! don't let thoughts like that disturb you,' said Macha, 'you are hale and strong and have many of the good things of life.'

'Well, I was thinking more of Orla than of myself. There will be no one left to care for her when we are gone.'

'That is true, for she shows no inclination to marry. She has rejected many suitors and dislikes the idea of settling down to married life. What about making arrangements for the great ball to which you intend to invite so many friends? Orla might choose a husband from among the guests there.'

'Oh, yes, I must see about preparing for the ball.'

'Here she comes,' said Macha, as Orla approached the house. 'How bright and beautiful she looks after her walk through the gardens.'

'Well, *a chailín*,' said the father, 'your mother and I have been speaking about the ball we intend to have in a few months' time.'

'Oh! Father, hurry, please, and make all arrangements. You know how much I love music and dancing.'

'Perhaps, Orla,' said Macha, 'you might choose a husband from among the gallant young men.'

'Oh! please, Mother dear, don't talk of such a thing. I am perfectly happy as I am with you and Father and Brid, my dear old nurse. Indeed, I have not the least desire to marry. I have never yet met the man I would like as a husband. The man I would marry must be rich, clever, handsome and of good family. In fact, he must be perfection.'

One of the greatest interests in Orla's life was looking after the flowers in the garden. She spent much of her time with Conaire, an old gardener who had been with the family for many years. A strong friendship existed between the girl and the old man. Suddenly Orla felt the first real sorrow of her life.

One morning she went to the gardens and found Conaire lying on the ground. He smiled faintly and in a moment he was dead. Orla mourned his loss greatly. 'I shall never find such a dear, loyal friend as Conaire,' she said. 'For his sake I will tend the flowers and plants he loved so well.'

Shortly after Conaire's death a man came to the castle and asked to be hired to fill the place left vacant by the old man's death.

'You are young and strong,' said the head gardener, 'but your hands do not show any signs of hard work.'

'They have been idle,' said the stranger, 'but that does not mean they will be unable to do the work required.'

'Very well, take this spade and show what you can do.' The gardener went away and left the new man to begin his work.

After a while Orla came into the garden. She saw the strange workman. He was labouring hard but did not seem to be making much progress.

'Perhaps,' said Orla, 'if you had a larger spade you would do better. That one is too short for your height.' 'I fear,' she thought to herself, 'that man is not strong enough for the work, but he may improve with time. What beautiful hands he has! It seems a pity to spoil them.'

Next morning she paid her usual visit to the gardens. She went to the place where the young man was working.

He did not raise his head when he saw her approaching, but she noticed that he was breathing heavily and seemed tired and strained.

'Will you not rest for a moment?' she asked.

'Oh, no,' was his reply. 'I must continue what I have agreed to do.'

'But it is hard work in the great heat of the scorching sun.'

'Thanks for your consideration, kind lady, but I have agreed to do the work and am in duty bound to continue it.'

Orla returned to the house. She sought her faithful friend, Brid.

'Brid,' she said, 'will you bring a cool drink to the new man who is working in the garden. He is exhausted. I will wait here till you come back.'

Brid thought this was a strange request, but without making any remark she did as she was asked. She returned with the word that the man seemed almost worn out. 'Indeed,' said Brid, 'I think it strange that one like him should be doing such work.'

'That is my opinion, too, Brid. He looks to me like one who has been tenderly reared. I wonder is he a nobleman who has lost all his wealth.'

'Whatever he is, *asthore*, the work seems too much for the poor man.'

Next day Orla went again to the garden. The man did not see her approaching. When she came nearer she found

He wiped the perspiration from his brow

him leaning with one hand on the spade while with the other he wiped the perspiration from his brow. When he turned and saw her he bent his head as if to avoid speaking to her, and as she came nearer he hurried away.

'How tired and weary he is,' she thought. 'I hate to think of him trying to work when he seems almost unable to stand. Oh! if only I could help him!'

Next day she had a bad headache. She remained in her own room. The faithful Brid came to her.

'Rest now, *alanna*. The day is very hot. Don't stir out, but try to sleep and the headache will go away.'

'Wait a minute, Brid. Will you go to the gardens and come back and tell me if that poor man is still tired and overworked.'

Brid was astonished that Orla should still show such concern for the stranger, but she said she would do what her loved child wished. When she returned Orla asked anxiously:

'Is he better, Brid?'

'I don't know, *asthore*, for there is no sign of him in the garden and none of the men know where he is.'

To Brid's great surprise, Orla began to cry.

'What is the matter, *alanna*?' she asked.

'Oh! Brid, I fear he is very ill. I may never see him again.'

'But, *asthore*, why should you wish to see him again?'

'Because he was so brave and patient trying to work when he was almost worn out.'

'Well, he has stopped working now. Don't think of him any more.'

'I will think of him. I believe he is noble and good and I hate to think of him weary and sad.'

'Now, my dear, forget about him and you and I will keep silence about the whole affair.'

But Orla did not forget. 'Oh, how foolish I was to think I would never marry a poor man. I have seen the man I would take as a husband before all the men of the world.' Such were her thoughts when left alone.

Some miles from Orla's house there was a magnificent castle. In it lived an elderly gentleman named Conan. He was something of a recluse, but there was a strong friendship between him and Feilim though they seldom met. Conan had no living relative except a nephew named Oscar. Oscar paid short visits to him from time to time. Though the old man was solitary in his habits he had always a welcome for his nephew. They were very fond of each other.

Oscar happened to be staying in the castle when Feilim sent out the invitations to the ball. He received one.

'You will accept the invitation, Oscar, my boy, won't you?'

'Oh! yes, Uncle.'

'Perhaps you would be the successful suitor.'

'Oh! Uncle, why do you talk like that? You who never married.'

'No, my boy, I never married.'

'Why, Uncle?'

'The girl who would have been my wife died on our appointed wedding day.'

'Who was she, Uncle?'

'She was the sister of Feilim, my greatest friend. Orla was her name. My friend gave the name Orla to his daughter because, like his sister, she had golden hair. But no more of sorrow and regret. "Enjoy the springtime of love and youth." Now, with my blessing go to the ball and be happy.'

The time for the ball was now at hand. The banquet hall was a scene of great splendour. While the preparations were going on Orla was in her dressing-room. The faithful Brid was by her side.

'How beautiful you look, *asthore*,' she said. 'You should be very happy.'

'Oh! Brid, I wish I knew the fate of the poor gardener.'

'Put the thought of the gardener out of your mind, child. Just wait till you see all the fine young men who will be present tonight.'

Macha came into the room. 'Now, my child, try to please your father and me by choosing a husband from among the suitors.'

With music and dancing the hours sped on.

There was a lull in the enjoyment as Feilim rose to speak.

'I will now ask those who are suitors for my daughter to come forward.'

Just at that moment there was a great sensation at the back of the hall. A handsome young man entered in haste and came towards the place where Feilim stood. On seeing him Orla turned pale and almost lost consciousness. 'The gardener,' she murmured as she sank into a chair. For a moment there was silence. Then Feilim spoke.

'Welcome, Oscar, nephew of my dearest friend.'

'I ask pardon for my late and very informal entrance,' said the newcomer.

'Late or early, you are heartily welcome,' said Macha, as she went forward to greet him.

'My thanks for your kind words, dear lady. Now to account for my delay. I set out from my uncle's house in good time, but the driver of the carriage took a wrong turn and went many miles out of the way.'

All this time Orla looked on pale and trembling.

'What is the matter, my child?' asked Macha.

'Perhaps,' said Oscar, 'I can explain the cause of your daughter's agitation. I pray you listen just a while. During my visits to my uncle, I have seen the Lady Orla as she passed by in her carriage. She was quite unaware of my presence. From the moment my eyes beheld her I knew she was the one woman I would choose for my wife. I crave your patience my good listeners for just a little longer.'

'No patience is required,' said Feilim.

'Please tell the whole story,' Macha said.

'Well, when I received the invitation to this ball I

determined to try to win the lady's heart before I sought her hand in marriage. I believed her heart was full of unawakened affection and sympathy. I shall try to win her pity, thought I, for is not pity akin to love?'

'Please tell us your method of awakening sympathy,' said one of the suitors in a laughing tone.

'I worked in the gardens disguised as a labourer. I admit this was a strange way to seek to gain her affection. From the moment Orla and I met there was sympathy between us. She grieved to see me worn out and weary and tried, as far as possible, to help and cheer me. Remembering all this I dared to come here tonight. I know there are present more worthy suitors than I. May I ask the lady herself to deign to make the choice?'

For answer, Orla went towards the speaker and placed her hand in his. There were words of congratulation from all sides. Even the disappointed suitors seemed to share in the felicitations.

Oscar and Orla lived long and happily. They had many children. One of the joys of old Brid's life was to tell them stories. The one they liked best was the true one about the time Daddy became a gardener and got big blisters on his hands.

The Two Trees

Centuries and centuries ago there were two kings in Ireland who were great enemies. They were Niall, King of Leinster, and Fergal, King of Ulster. Niall had a daughter named Niav, Fergal a son named Oscar.

Oscar had among the nobles of the Court a very good and loyal friend. This was Crionna who had been his wise tutor.

One day he and the young prince were walking in a wood near the palace.

'Isn't it a great pity, Crionna,' said Oscar, 'that my father and King Niall are enemies?'

'Indeed it is,' replied Crionna, 'and they were one time such friends.'

'I have heard,' said Oscar, 'that it was a deceitful woman that caused the trouble between them.'

'Yes, the handsome but treacherous Maeve pretended to be in love with each one and roused jealousy and hatred in both hearts. The extraordinary thing is that though both made happy marriages afterwards the old bitterness and resentment remained.'

'My mother,' said Oscar, 'was always sad to think of

the bad feeling between the two. She was so fond of Ailibhe, King Niall's wife. I sometimes think the brooding sorrow hastened her early death.'

'Perhaps it did, but she was never very strong.'

By this time they had come to a place where a solitary yew tree grew near a small lake.

'I believe,' said Oscar, 'there is a story connected with that yew tree. You remember, Crionna, that as a child I often wanted to hear it but you said it was too sad to tell.'

'Well, I will tell it to you now,' said Crionna.

'A young chieftain named Baile set out from Ulster to meet Aillin, the daughter of the King of Leinster, whom he loved. On the way he was told that the princess had been killed whereupon he fell dead and the yew tree grew on his grave.'

'That is a sad tale.'

'Yes, and there is a similar story about an apple tree in the orchard of the King of Leinster. When his daughter Aillin heard that Baile had died she too fell dead and an apple tree grew over her grave.'

'They are strange stories,' said Oscar.

'Yes,' said Crionna, 'but more wonderful still, there is a prophecy that those trees will yet bring love and peace to other hearts.'

'It seems strange,' said Oscar, 'how that should come about, but we must now return to the palace as it is time for the mid-day meal.'

Oscar could not sleep that night. When he dozed he

seemed to see the yew tree close beside him. He had only a few snatches of sleep. At last he rose and went to the wood. The moon was shining brightly. A light breeze stirred the leaves of the yew. Their gentle movement seemed like a lullaby. He lay down under the tree and was soon in a sound sleep. In a dream he heard a voice that seemed to come from beneath the tree. These words reached his ear:

Here beneath the yew
   Was laid a lover true
Who could no longer stay
   When love had passed away.
E'er the day will break
   In the nearby lake
A shadow you will see
   Of Niav your bride to be.

Oscar awoke suddenly. He went to the side of the lake. There by the light of the moon he saw in the water the face of a beautiful girl. Even as he gazed the vision faded.

The first thing he did next morning was to seek out Crionna.

'I had a wonderful dream last night,' he said.

'Tell me about it, my son.'

When Crionna heard all, he said more to himself than to Oscar, 'I wonder will the prophecy come true?'

'I must find that apple tree,' said Oscar. 'I will set out at once to seek it.'

'If you do there is a long and perilous journey before you.'

'No matter how dangerous it is I will undertake it.'

'It will be very hard. You can take neither horse nor carriage but must travel on foot without any companion.'

'I am prepared to travel alone, no obstacle will prevent me from going.'

'Well, if you are brave and persevering you will succeed.

'You must take provisions with you and even if these provisions are nearly gone before you reach the end of your journey you must not refuse food to any one who asks it.

'One more word. No matter what sounds you may hear do not turn your head to look back. Keep moving on looking straight before you.'

Next morning at dawn Oscar set out on his journey. He had walked many miles when he heard the sound of the sweetest music close behind him. He was about to turn round when he remembered Crionna's warning. He walked on looking straight before him. Then the wind seemed to whisper in his ear:

No music sweet your course can stay
Fair fortune's star shines on your way.

He sat down near a stream to eat some of the food he had brought with him. After a little while he started on his travels again.

The day was now very warm. As he walked along he

felt as if a rod of fire was placed on his back. Remembering Crionna's warning he pushed on bravely without looking back.

Again the wind seemed to whisper:

No scorching sun can you dismay
Fair fortune's star shines on your way.

As night came on he slept in the shelter of a great rock. In the morning after he had walked some distance he heard the trampling of feet and the loud bellowing of a bull approaching from behind him. In terror he was about to turn his head but remembering in time he went on.

Again he heard the voice in the wind:

Your courage over fear holds sway
Fair fortune's star shines on your way.

Bravely he travelled on till at last he came in sight of the wall surrounding the King's palace. His provisions were now nearly finished. Before entering the grounds he sat down to rest on a great stone close by the gate leading to the orchard. He was about to eat the portion of the food that remained when a wretched looking woman wrapped in a long cloak approached him.

'Share your food with me, good stranger,' she said, 'I am starving.'

Hungry though he was he gave her all that remained of the food. The woman took it eagerly and went swiftly away.

Oscar was now almost worn out. He determined to rest a while before going through the gate into the orchard.

Though it was mid-September the day was very hot. The sun was shedding golden gleams over the gardens surrounding the palace. The orchard looked particularly beautiful with the ripening fruit showing through the green leaves. Suddenly the silence was broken by the light footfall of a girl who came out of the palace. She moved slowly. She was tired, having been at a ball the previous night. Under an apple tree she stopped and thought to herself.

'This tree has stood here for ages and still seems young and fresh. Nurse always said there is a sad story about it. I love the old tree. I will rest a while under its boughs just as I used to do when I was a little child.'

Soon she was asleep. In her dreams she heard a voice saying:

Underneath the apple tree
　Is my lowly bed;
Earth held no charm nor joy for me
　When he I loved lay dead.

Better fate be yours than mine
　See your Oscar pictured here;
Happiness and peace be thine
　With him to you so dear.

As the last words died away she saw in her dream a young handsome prince standing before her. She awoke with a start.

At the same moment Oscar entered the orchard and went towards the apple tree.

Both stood in amazement gazing at each other.

Niav!

Oscar!

For a moment they remained silent gazing at each other. Then Oscar said:

'You are Niav, daughter of King Niall.'

'Yes,' replied Niav, 'and you are Oscar, son of King Fergal.'

Just then a voice was heard calling, 'Princess Niav, come, come, the Queen awaits you.'

It was Aoife, Niav's special attendant, who came towards them. She stood still in astonishment looking at the young pair. Then Niav spoke,

'Yes, Aoife, Prince Oscar and I will follow you indoors at once.'

Niav, accompanied by Oscar, went to the room where the Queen Ailibhe was waiting for her.

When Ailibhe heard of their meeting and of their dreams she was, of course, very much surprised.

'Was it not very strange, Mother, that Oscar and I should have had those wonderful dreams?'

'It was indeed,' the Queen replied, 'but I had often heard the story of the apple tree.'

'And,' said Oscar, 'a wise man at my father's court told me the tale about the yew tree in our grounds.'

'I hope,' said Niav, 'that my father and Oscar's father will now become friends.'

Both stood in amazement gazing at each other

'Your father is absent from home and will not be back for some days. I would like Oscar to remain here till he returns.'

'Then perhaps,' said Oscar, 'the old quarrel might be ended.'

'Not so easily, I fear,' said the Queen, 'but I have a plan in my mind which may make the two kings friends again.'

'Oh! anything that would heal the old heart wounds would be welcome,' Niav said.

'Your father and I hope soon to call the nobles together so that you might choose a husband.'

'But, Mother, I have already chosen Oscar.'

'Patience, Niav. I will arrange to have this assembly held on the night of your father's return. At the gathering he will give you a stone cup which you will present to the man of your choice. By giving you the cup your father has pledged his word that you are free to choose whom you will. He cannot withdraw that word.'

'Oh,' said Oscar, 'I wish my poor mother could be present to obtain my father's consent with such ease.'

'Your mother and I loved each other. I know she would be happy to think the old quarrel was ended. Ended too by the marriage of her loved son with the child of her devoted friend.'

Oscar and Niav passed many hours together. Their favourite walk was through the orchard and they never passed the apple tree without thinking of the poor princess who was buried there so long ago.

One day as they were standing near the tree Niav said, 'I would like to see the yew tree.'

'You will soon see it, I hope,' said Oscar. 'I have sent word to Crionna to tell my father all that has happened. It is better he should hear all from Crionna than from anyone else. I hope he will not come here till after you have given me the cup.'

On the morning of the day fixed for the assembly, King Niall returned. The Queen thought it was better that he and Oscar should not meet till after the festival had begun.

That night the hall was a scene of splendour. Music added to the beauty. Many lovely ladies in magnificent dresses were present. No one among them was more beautiful than Niav.

When the enjoyment was at its highest the King rose up on his throne and said,

'Let the princess present this cup to him she would choose for her husband.'

Two attendants advanced to the throne, one bearing a goblet of water, the other a stone cup. When the cup was filled the King took it and handed it to his daughter saying,

'May good fortune direct your choice.'

Niav, with blushing face, advanced towards Oscar. He went on his knee to receive the cup.

Cries of joy and congratulations came from all sides. Then the King spoke,

'I wish to hear the name of him whom my daughter has chosen.'

'I am Oscar, son of Fergal, King of Ulster.'

'Yes,' said the Queen, speaking rapidly and with decision, 'he has received the cup. You cannot withdraw your consent to the marriage.'

The King was silent for a moment. Suddenly there was a swift movement among the guests. Fergal, with Crionna, had entered the hall. He spoke in anger:

'I understand that the Princess Niav, your daughter, has chosen my son to be her husband. Have you forgotten that you and I are enemies?'

'No, but I gave my word that my daughter could marry the man to whom she gave the cup. I have in this way given my consent to the marriage.'

'I gave no cup, I will not give my consent,' declared Fergal angrily.

At this stage great excitement was caused among the guests by the appearance of a poor ragged woman. The guards and guests were so much astonished that they allowed her to force her way to the throne. There she stood. She threw back the hood which had hidden her face. Both kings recognized her. Both uttered the same word, 'Maeve.'

Oscar knew the voice to be that of her who had asked him for food. The woman spoke,

'I have come to bring peace where I brought strife, love where I brought hatred. You see me now a poor wretch from whom every good thing has gone, beauty, wealth, friends, happiness.'

Falling on her knees she continued,

'Oh, end this bitter quarrel and let the love of the young people be the healing power that will lead to happiness for you and them and forgiveness for me.'

After exchanging glances Fergal and Niall went towards each other. They clasped hands amid a scene of tumultuous rejoicing among the guests.

Maeve was about to leave the hall when Ailibhe gently led her to a seat.

'If you will make your home in the palace,' she said, 'you will have ease and comfort for the rest of your life.'

So saying she called two of her maidens to bring Maeve away.

After all the guests had departed the two kings talked together. To the great delight of all, Fergal with Crionna agreed to remain at Niall's Court till the wedding preparations were complete.

In a short time the marriage took place and ever after there was strong friendship between the two kings.

Sinéad de Valera
Irish Fairy Tales £2.99

From the land of pixies, fairies, witches and druids, twelve strange
and wonderful stories of sorcery and magical spells – from the evil
fairy who could take the form of any animal, to the giant who stole
the king's crown ...

Grant Campbell
Scottish Hauntings £1.99

A chilling collection of hauntings from a country steeped in legends
and ghost stories. Grant Campbell brings to light many stories which
until now have only been talked about in hushed voices. The stories
are gathered from every region of Scotland – a land full of magic and
mystery.

Antoine de Saint-Exupery
The Little Prince £4.99

The little Prince comes to earth to learn the secret of what is really
important in life, and he tells an air pilot in the Sahara Desert what
he has learned, in stories about the planet where he lives – stories
about a haughty flower, his fight with the bad seeds, and other
planets and their rulers.

Judy Blume
Are you there God? It's me, Margaret £2.99

'I just told my mother I wanted a bra. Please help me grow, God.
You know where. Oh please, God, I just want to be normal . . .'

There just doesn't seem to be anyone around that Margaret can talk
to – *really* talk about the problems of growing up – boys, school
and parents. So Margaret chats to God about her troubles, hoping
He can help her find the answers.

It's Not the End of the World £2.99

Karen is twelve and her world is crumbling. First of all her mother
and father were arguing all the time – then her father moved out and
didn't come back. Now he's going to Las Vegas to fix up a divorce.
Karen's new friend Val has been through it too . . . But maybe Karen
and her brother Jeff and baby sister Amy can somehow stop it
happening – or maybe they just don't stand a chance.

Then Again, Maybe I Won't £2.99

Tony is thirteen and he's just moved house. Now he lives in the best
part of Long Island, surrounded by luxury homes and swimming
pools. Next door there's Joel who's a dab hand at shoplifting. Joel's
older sister Lisa gets undressed every night with the lights on and
the curtains open. Tony's mother thinks everything's swell on Long
Island. She wants Tony to be just like the kids next door – or does
she?

Betsy Byars
The Not-Just-Anybody Family £2.99

Boy Breaks Into City Jail

It made all the headlines when Vern broke *into* prison, but what would you do if your grandpa was in jail? The Blossoms had no doubts. Since they couldn't get Pap out, Maggie and Vern had to get in. A little unusual, perhaps, but as Maggie said, 'We Blossoms have never been just "anybody".'

This is the first adventure for the Blossoms – Pap, Vern, Maggie Junior and Mud the dog. They're a family you won't forget.

Lorna Hill
A Dream of Sadler's Wells £2.99

This is the first of the Wells series in which we meet Veronica, who is determined to become a dancer. She is torn away from London and her ballet classes and sent to live with unsympathetic relations in Northumberland, but she manages to overcome all sorts of setbacks and finally reaches her audition for the Royal Ballet School at Sadler's Wells.

All Pan books are available at your local bookshop or newsagent, or can be ordered direct from the publisher. Indicate the number of copies required and fill in the form below.

Send to: **CS Department, Pan Books Ltd., P.O. Box 40, Basingstoke, Hants. RG21 2YT.**

or phone: 0256 469551 (Ansaphone), quoting title, author and Credit Card number.

Please enclose a remittance* to the value of the cover price plus: 60p for the first book plus 30p per copy for each additional book ordered to a maximum charge of £2.40 to cover postage and packing.

*Payment may be made in sterling by UK personal cheque, postal order, sterling draft or international money order, made payable to Pan Books Ltd.

Alternatively by Barclaycard/Access:

Card No.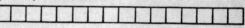

Signature:

Applicable only in the UK and Republic of Ireland.

While every effort is made to keep prices low, it is sometimes necessary to increase prices at short notice. Pan Books reserve the right to show on covers and charge new retail prices which may differ from those advertised in the text or elsewhere.

NAME AND ADDRESS IN BLOCK LETTERS PLEASE:

....

Name ——————————————————————————

Address ——————————————————————————

——————————————————————————

——————————————————————————

——————————————————————————

3/87